THE OTHER SENSES

OTHER LOTUS TITLES

Ajit Bhattacharjea	*Sheikh Mohammad Abdullah: Tragic Hero of Kashmir*
Anil Dharker	*Icons: Men & Women Who Shaped Today's India*
Aitzaz Ahsan	*The Indus Saga: The Making of Pakistan*
Alam Srinivas & TR Vivek	*IPL: The Inside Story*
Amarinder Singh	*The Last Sunset: The Rise & Fall of the Lahore Durbar*
Amir Mir	*The True Face of Jehadis: Inside Pakistan's Terror Networks*
Ashok Mitra	*The Starkness of It*
H.L.O. Garrett	*The Trial of Bahadur Shah Zafar*
Hussain Zaidi	*Dongri to Dubai: Six Decades of Mumbai Mafia*
Kiran Maitra	*Marxism in India: From Decline to Debacle*
M.B. Naqvi	*Pakistan at Knife's Edge*
M.J. Akbar	*Byline*
M.J. Akbar	*Blood Brothers: A Family Saga*
Maj. Gen. Ian Cardozo	*Param Vir: Our Heroes in Battle*
Maj. Gen. Ian Cardozo	*The Sinking of INS Khukri: What Happened in 1971*
Madhu Trehan	*Tehelka as Metaphor*
Masood Hyder	*October Coup: A Memoir of the Struggle for Hyderabad*
Nayantara Sahgal (ed.)	*Before Freedom: Nehru's Letters to His Sister*
Nilima Lambah	*A Life Across Three Continents*
Peter Church	*Added Value: The Life Stories of Indian Business Leaders*
Salman Akhtar	*Book of Emotions*
Sharmishta Gooptu and Boria Majumdar (eds)	*Revisiting 1857: Myth, Memory, History*
Shashi Joshi	*The Last Durbar*
Shashi Tharoor & Shaharyar M. Khan	*Shadows Across the Playing Field*
Shrabani Basu	*Spy Princess: The Life of Noor Inayat Khan*
Shyam Bhatia	*Goodbye Shahzadi: A Political Biography*
Vir Sanghvi	*Men of Steel: Indian Business Leaders in Candid Conversations*

FORTHCOMING TITLES

Alam Srinivas	*Women Icons*
Monisha Rajesh	*Around India in 80 Trains*

THE OTHER SENSES

AN INSPIRING TRUE STORY OF A VISUALLY IMPAIRED WOMAN AND HER ROAD TO SUCCESS

Preeti Monga

LOTUS COLLECTION
ROLI BOOKS

Lotus Collection

First published in 2012

The Lotus Collection
An imprint of
Roli Books Pvt. Ltd
M-75, Greater Kailash II Market, New Delhi 110 048
Phone: ++91 (011) 40682000
Fax: ++91 (011) 2921 7185
E-mail: info@rolibooks.com
Website: www.rolibooks.com
Also at Bangalore, Chennai, & Mumbai

Layout: Sanjeev Mathpal
Production: Shaji Sahadevan
Cover design: Bonita Vaz-Shimray

ISBN: 978-81-7436-908-6

Typeset in ITC Galliard by Roli Books Pvt. Ltd
Printed at Sanat Printers, Haryana.

Dedicated to all

who have made me

and

this book possible.

On a chilly Saturday evening in December 2007, we arrived at EDM Mall in East Delhi, where we were to watch a much talked about Hindi movie. Jumping out of our newly bought car, my husband Ashwani and I raced cheerfully towards the multiplex, when we plunged headlong into another of our humorous, on road, episodes.

The piercing breeze charged our energy and sense of excitement, as we sped into the warm ambience of the multiplex. Once indoors, Ashwani swiftly handed me over to the lady deputed at the security check counter near the entrance, and hurried through with his own, in order to return at the earliest to escort me to the auditorium. It was nearly time for the film to start, and as we had been caught in an unexpected traffic jam, we raced, arm in arm, at full speed towards the elevator.

As we reached, lo and behold, it suddenly came to a grinding halt, nearly tripping most people in mid-passage! Taken by surprise and disappointed at the evident delay, we began scouting around for an alternative, but before we could move away from the elevator, we noticed that the security guard from the counter we had left behind was approaching us with an expression of acute concern. 'I have switched off the elevator for madam,' he said, pointing in my direction with the greatest sympathy, 'I saw that madam is holding you and walking as if there is something wrong with her legs; I thought that she would not be able to jump on to the running stairs'. At this, chuckling, we reassured the kind and thoughtful gentleman that all was well with my legs, and to wipe off the confused look on his face, informed him of my blindness, which made holding hands a necessity!

This is not the first time my long, shapely, and reasonably fit legs have fallen under suspicion.

It is, however, intriguing, to note why or how people suspect the reliability of my legs. On one occasion, we were on a trip to Ajmer in Rajasthan. I was switching escorts between Ashwani, Prithvi, my nephew, Rachna, my sister-in-law, and my brother, Sandy. When we reached the celebrated and historic Ajmer Sharif shrine, here too the ability of my legs was once more questioned, and this, while I was energetically climbing up and down the ancient stairs to touch various objects in order to be able to *see* them. It must be a bit puzzling I expect. As it is said, I don't look blind! There must certainly be some degree of truth in this, because on the following day, we were at Jaipur City Palace, where I once again became the cause of a heated argument between fellow tourists and the security guards. I had obtained special permission to enter the cordoned-off area to be able to see with my hands, the world's largest silver water pitcher displayed there. Spotting Prithvi and me sort of messing around on forbidden ground with the silver pitcher, a group of tourists jumped the rope barrier to join us. They were immediately stopped by the security guard, which sparked a verbal battle. 'Are those two your relatives, or have they bribed you to allow them in?' They screamed, without giving him an opportunity to respond, 'We too wish to go and touch that thing there; why are you preventing us and permitting those two in?' The guard at last got a word in, informing them of my inability to see the pitcher without touching it due to my blindness. Paying no heed to the poor guard's explanation, they argued on, 'Even we want to touch and see it; you simply must allow us too. Anyhow, we don't believe you; she looks fine to us, and there is something fishy going on here.' Finally, my family stepped in and salvaged the situation, while I surveyed the beautiful silver pitcher, guided by Prithvi, marvelling at the huge piece of art, and tracing my fingers over the exquisitely carved handles and lid.

I can't move on without relating just one more of the many hilarious incidents that I have experienced. The other evening, I was travelling back alone by air to Delhi from Ahmedabad, when the young ground assistant of Jet Airways, deputed to help me, trotted off briskly with my hand luggage tugging at the arm of the driver who had brought me to the airport, rather than mine. Later, when the confusion had been sorted out, she sweetly muttered to me, 'Madam, I was completely baffled when I saw the two of you standing as you have such a wonderful dress sense; I could never have imagined that it could have been you who needed assistance. I thought the man with you was blind. I profusely apologize for the goof-up.'

The matter gets even more comic when people like Mr Khushwant Singh also managed to fall into the trap. The story goes like this: I happened to visit Mr Singh and to avoid the obvious confusion, I took the precaution of mentioning over the phone that I was visually impaired.

When we arrived at his Sujan Singh Park house in New Delhi for the meeting, we walked apprehensively towards the beautiful ground floor apartment along the well-kept driveway, to the handsomely carved front door. My companion was already a little scared at the idea of having to accompany me to meet Mr Khushwant Singh. For my part, I was deeply honoured and extremely excited at just the thought that someone of Mr Singh's stature had found the time from his very hectic schedule to see me. Well, my excitement was further heightened when the door opened, and our high-profile host himself greeted us with an enthusiastic 'Come on in!' Before I could say anything, he gallantly slipped his arm into that of my quaking companion and off they went through the entrance hallway. Realizing what had happened, I was somewhat taken aback, utterly confused, and a little concerned at this strange occurrence, aware of my little friend's trepidation about my current mission. Then, as I heard Mr Singh say to the little lady he was escorting away, 'I am so happy you could come and join me for a cup of tea, Preeti,' the mystery was resolved.

As have many others, Mr Khushwant Singh had also taken the bait, mistaken Aditi for Preeti, and was only ever so harmlessly playing the perfect host by trying to make 'Preeti' welcome and comfortable! Aditi, for her part, had been gripped by a turbulent fear that engulfed her entire being, having from the very outset viewed this venture as a visit to the lion's den. Her fears had after all been confirmed, she must have thought, and gripped by a paralytic shock because she could not even find her voice to correct the mistaken identity. Once I recovered from my initial surprise, shaking with amusement, I called after the almost disappearing pair, 'Mr Singh,' I giggled, 'Preeti has been abandoned right here at your doorstep. It's I who needs to be guided indoors, not her; she can get around perfectly well on her own,' politely adding a 'thanks'. A sudden silence followed, as Mr Singh swung around, quickly delinked his arm from Aditi's, and raced to the open doorway where I was stranded, and then gallantly taking mine, smiling sheepishly, escorted me into his royal drawing room. 'I never thought I could make such a blunder,' he admitted, 'you are one of the very few who has got the better of me. It is usually the other way around.'

We spent the evening sipping lovely hot tea and chatting about many things, but he kept saying all along, 'I can't get over the fact that I could have been fooled like this! I must write about you in my column and pay you a tribute.' It is indeed a great honour to appear in Mr Khushwant Singh's 'With Malice Towards One and All' column, which is published in the *Hindustan Times* every Saturday. Although the idea of figuring in it appeared to be a real treat, I felt a touch of discomfort at the controversies that accompanied this. My expression must have revealed how I felt, because he immediately said, 'I promise to write nothing controversial about you, because it is only admiration that I feel looking at you. There is something very special lurking behind the well-painted nails and the glittering little nose pin you wear! I can quite easily guess what is going through your mind. Believe me Preeti, my dear, I have women chasing me to write about them, and I admire you more for having second thoughts about it. That only reinforces my feeling that I must really honour you in this way, my dear.'

I feel so good and yet so muddled at the thought that I don't come across as a blind person, and this may very well be why people seem to feel a sense of displeasure at my style of walking arm in arm. They ever so often push their way towards my escort and me and force their way between us as if to say, 'This wont do'.

As I sit at my computer this morning, writing about my life experiences, I am unable to resist the temptation of drawing for you the glorious pictures stored away in the closet of my reminiscence. I therefore surrender to the flight of my fingers on the keyboard as they paint with the colours of words, images of the glorious albums stored away, beginning with my oldest collections!

Ever so often in the morning, when my mother stood cooking, I would find myself perched, swinging my legs, on top of the wooden chest in the kitchen, which, to the then three-year-old me, inferred the thrill of being suspended in mid-air. These moments were probably some of the happiest ones in my life, and I still cherish memories of the mouth-watering aroma emitted by the round, white *chapatis* cooking over on the *tava*, and the old-fashioned pressure stove.

The next glance inside the closet of my memory reveals our house with dark wooden flooring, topped with a slanting metal roof, perched on a hillside in Simla, a picture-book town in the heart of the Himalayas. My mention of the roof and floor here has a deeper meaning than just the aesthetics, as both were made out of materials that made sound. At that time, however, we were unaware that I could not see much with my eyes and that therefore, sounds, smells, and touch would play a big role in my little life. The sound of footsteps on the wooden floor and the pitter-patter of raindrops on the metal roof must have conveyed a secure and cozy comfort.

Playing in the snow-covered courtyard and frequent visits to the ice-skating rink never failed to delight me! However, at the ice-skating rink, it was the goodies I went after and never really mastered the sport! My inhibition about skating was further bolstered when one evening, I was accidentally thrown off balance by a stream of enthusiastic skaters. Caught unaware amidst zipping men and women, I lay stretched out on the cold, hard ice, panic-stricken, shrieking in terror, and wildly waving my short arms to attract the attention of the non-stop 'moonlight' skaters! The next imprint in my album of memories depicts me waddling up the snow-covered restaurant staircase to a soothing treat of a comforting hotdog.

Then there are memories of the winters we spent away from the grand town of Simla to holiday in the capital city of Delhi with family and friends. These were trips which I don't remember having particularly looked forward to, because being in Simla was much more fun than being surrounded by the hustle and bustle of Delhi.

From Simla we normally took a bus up to Kalka, as the narrow-gauge train took far too long. From there, we caught the Kalka Mail which brought us to Delhi overnight. Once we got out of the train in one piece, struggling between rushing travellers and shoving of baggage, the milling crowd with its deafening sound never failed to drown me. As I write about my experience of arriving at the Delhi station, the vivid memory of a million needles pricking my body inflicted by the heat brings back to me the same feeling of suffocation to this day. Gripping my mother's hand with all my might, I would drag myself out of the chaotic railway station and into a rattling yellow and black Ambassador taxi, to arrive at my grandparents' home in South Patel Nagar for the vacation.

Once home, the sight of my grandfather, a chubby Sikh gentleman with a distinguished milk-white beard and a white turban, gradually assuaged my dampened spirits. My father's dad, who I remember ever so fondly, loved eating good food and usually went about his daily business in an enormous rush. I also cannot ever forget my short and tubby grandmother, grumbling and muttering away for no apparent reason, while her favourite hobby of washing every piece of cloth in sight, truly made me wonder! She would be in her element every morning, sitting on a small wooden stool, with the bathroom door wide open, steeped in the foaming washing soap, thumping away at her washing dressed in her 'swimsuit'. This 'swimsuit', was her short saree blouse and with it, she would wear her long knee-length underwear, which would leave her arms and legs bare, to allow total freedom and agility to enjoy her hour with her washing.

The rest of the joint family living in this house comprised two of my father's brothers, my aunt (my father's brother's wife), and their two daughters. I quite enjoyed listening in on the grown-ups chatter, but the shrieking little kids, my uncle's two daughters and little Sandy, were never my cup of tea. They would constantly play what I thought were silly games, and to top it all, kept nagging me to join them. Although I used all the possible means I could to dissuade the brats, they persisted in pestering me to join their ridiculous games, and when I ignored them, they begged my mother to command me to comply with their wishes. My irritation with my little brother and cousins were further exacerbated because Mummy ensured that I accept their invitation, which meant having to waste my time playing foolish games rather than engaging in my favourite pastime of listening to grown-up talk. What I did however enjoy in Delhi, was riding around in its double-decker buses and roaming about its lush green parks and busy shopping areas.

Following our stay in Delhi, we normally went to my maternal grandparents' house for the rest of the vacation, which was always like a dream come true, as my maternal grandfather had a transferable job, and we had the opportunity of seeing different places each time we visited them.

There, I felt like a queen basking in the unconditional doting of my grandparents and grand aunt, and in addition, the attention lavished upon us by the domestic staff. Loads of good food, lots of new places to visit; flittering about like a free, yet well-protected little bird.

I greatly admired my maternal grandfather (I called him Papa), with his smart police uniform and the stout wooden stick he carried; not ever did I miss the chance of getting my small fingers around this stick, to flourish it around, feeling like the ruler of the world!

Also, riding around the gorgeous countryside in Papa's jeep while he went about his official business was great fun. One such vacation lasted for over six months because Daddy had gone to the United States on a long official duty, and Mummy with Sandy and me were to spend most of the time with them.

Luckily for me, during these six months, Papa was transferred to three different places, and we travelled through most of the picturesque state of Himachal Pradesh nestling in the Himalayas. Fortunately, at this time, I still had some of my sight and I was able to see the landscape and other large things around me. I remember seeing colours, shapes, mountains and rivers, waterfalls and structures, the blue sky strewn with clouds by day and sprinkled with the glittering stars by night! Even today, as I focus on the canvas of memory, vivid is the sight of the twinkling fireflies flying about in the darkness of the cool nights, looking like the stars playing hide-and-seek in the jungle surrounding our house. On this same canvas are imprinted pictures of the beautiful little waterfalls splashing frothily down the mountain slopes into crystal clear pools lined with coloured pebbles. I remember imagining fairies and elves just beyond my field of vision, flittering about the pretty scene, waiting to love and cuddle me at the first possible opportunity. I also recall, the brilliantly coloured flowers perched upon their stems, me leaning over them with my nose, virtually within this wondrous miracle of nature, breathing in the enchanting perfume, when inevitably something would crawl up or flutter in my face and I would rush off vigorously, rubbing at the inflicted area, shrieking and trembling. Later, I would discover to my discomfiture, that the little monsters that had petrified me were none more than innocent butterflies and ladybirds only saying a polite 'hello' to their co-admirer. Although I was immensely scared of all crawlers and flutterers, nothing dissuaded me from returning to admire the enchanting plants and flowers. Within me, there must have surged a desire to capture the beauty and colours of the world to savour in my reminiscence before the lens of my natural camera, defused forever.

I was most fortunately my parent's adored first-born, even though a girl child. I say this because even today, in our part of the world, a boy child is the much preferred option. Mohini, my mother, was at that time in her early twenties, a beautiful, tall, and talented woman, and my father, Charanjit too was a handsome man of medium height in his late twenties. They were married in September 1956, when Mohini was just nineteen and Charanjit, twenty-six. My mother had completed her graduation and held a bachelor's degree in arts and Charanjit held a bachelor's degree in science, coupled with a degree in electrical engineering.

My father worked with the Central Water Power Commission, while my mother chose to take up the challenging role of a homemaker. Together, they made a handsome couple sharing love, admiration, and respect for each other, and their obvious devotion to each other was the envy of many. The first year of their married life was spent in Ajmer and then they moved to Simla.

In April 1959, their rosy-cheeked baby daughter, whom they named Preeti, arrived into their little heaven. After a patient wait of nearly ten months of pregnancy, on 22 April, Mohini was summoned to the hospital for a cesarean delivery, when it suddenly dawned upon me that I had better be off into the world before they hurled me out with knives and forks. My grandparents were there to greet me along with Mummy, and soon, Daddy had arrived too. I was welcomed like royalty, as I topped the list of grandchildren.

My naming ceremony took place at the famous Golden Temple, and as luck would have it, the handwritten Guru Granth Sahab was especially utilized for the purpose. The day I was taken to the gurdwara, the letter that was inscribed on the board for the first syllable for my name was 'kh'. However, my parents were unable to think of a pleasing name with that letter. The head priest was then requested to reopen the Granth Sahab and give them an alternative syllable. This was not possible, the priest told my parents, because the Granth Sahab in the main gurdwara is only opened for the 'Hukam Nama' (the first lines inscribed on the randomly opened page of the Guru Granth Sahab) early each morning, adopting the first syllable as the first letter for the baby's name, and cannot be done at will. This left my parents with very little choice, other than going to another gurdwara, which would deprive their little one of the privilege of being named at this important shrine.

My grandfather then revealed his official identity (he was at that time the superintendent of police of the city, a very important and respected position) and once again requested the priests to find a way of achieving our aim of having my naming ceremony at this holy shrine. The disclosure paid off, and the head priest led the way upstairs to the precious handwritten Guru Granth Sahab and performed the ceremony. Out came the letter 'P', and immediately, my mother named me 'Preeti', which means 'love', and I have never been denied that emotion ever since.

My grandmother had however, at that very instance, decided to call me 'Penny', as this was the name recommended by her sons (my maternal uncles), who had been away from home studying and then later working in England from their teenage years. Sadly, eight months after my birth, my dearest grandmother suddenly left all of us forever to reside in her heavenly abode and in her memory, I became 'Penny' to everyone, and today, it is my nick name, with 'Preeti' as my recognized first name.

In the days that followed, the heat and discomfort that goes with the summer in the plains of north India mounted with its usual fury. 'Now that little Penny is almost three weeks old, I think you better take her home, away from this scorching heat and into the comfort of the hills,' my grandfather thoughtfully suggested to my mother. 'Before you go, however, let me consult the doctor to find out if she can have her inoculations before you two leave,' he added, 'so you have no problems managing on your own.' The doctor agreed to administer the inoculations right away. This was done, including the smallpox shot. As is usual, the following day, I developed a fever as a natural reaction. Curiously however, the fever exceeded the expected duration and was soon followed by an angry red rash, which covered my entire body, and was most acute over my eyes, causing them to swell and become very red and inflamed. A severe allergy to one of the vaccines administered was diagnosed, which disappeared within a brief period with the appropriate medication. Then I was whirled away to the cool comfort of the mountains!

My infancy blossomed in the cradle of my caring parents assisted by Tulsi (a highly trained caregiver, who only looked after babies up to the age of two years). She ensured that I had absolutely no occasion to be unhappy. I only cried if I was somehow dislodged from Mummy's lap, and Tulsi's loving command to her was to keep me right there, while she undertook most of the housework.

My first birthday saw me taking my first independent steps. I had bloomed into a gentle, good-natured and obedient little girl, who clung to her parents and asked unlimited questions. Daddy's blissful good night ritual of putting me to bed relating the story of the lion and the goat or the birdie and the crow, laced with the lullabies of the tiny bird while going to sleep, vividly remains with me.

The sprawling playground in front of our house in Simla with a huge flat stone was to me, my private fairyland where I dreamt of 'Little Miss Moffet' being frightened away by the spider. I spent sunny mornings carrying toys in and out of this 'Fairyland', and in the winters, played with the soft, cold snow.

Life was blissful, basking in the comfort of being the princess of my world; everything was just as it should have been. The only conceivable source of lamentation was the delay, if at all, of milk and biscuits whenever I awoke. It remains the same today; I am never peppy without my biscuits and tea each morning.

Well, when I was about three, my cloud nine quivered with unwelcome thunder with the discovery that I would soon have to share my hitherto exclusive world with a sibling. Why should I give away my queendom to someone else? All that I possessed, including Mummy and Daddy, would soon be divided, or would possibly be taken over by the new arrival.

I must have given this news deep consideration and come to the conclusion that perhaps a baby sister could prove to be a good playmate, and I brought myself round to actually accepting the idea. However, the certainty of having a baby sister got diluted as every time the cleaning woman came to the house with the constant and repetitive blessing to my mother: 'May God give you a boy, my dear!' This was, to me, utterly unacceptable. Boys, I knew for certain, were rough creatures and this one would definitely hit me. Therefore, whenever I heard the poor old lady showering blessings on my mother, I would retort with: 'If and if a boy comes, remember your other eye will also go blind!' Alas, none of that worked: the boy came along, her good eye remained unscathed. Soon, I began loving my little brother Sandy, and continue to remain ever grateful for the poor old lady's fearless blessings!

Now it was time or me to go to school. Auckland House was the school I was sent to, where the kind-hearted, silver-haired Miss Atkins, was my headmistress. As my new life at school unfolded, I experienced a lot of excitement, a twinge of fear, and a great many new people and happenings occupied my days. Although I can't remember having any particular friends at school, walking up and down the well-lit corridors and wide wooden staircases, dipping my fingers in the bowl of holy water outside the school Chapel seemed to be fun. I remember sitting, holding my breath with sheer excitement, in the much too huge hall crammed with chairs, eagerly awaiting the commencement of the puppet show, while longing that one of those little things would emerge from behind the curtains to sit with me. Then there was the fancy dress show, which saw me on the stage as Little Red Riding Hood, where I walked as if the wolf was really following me to grab my basket of flowers and cakes! The same stage awarded me the opportunity of acting as a soldier's wife in a musical play, 'Soldier, soldier, will you marry me...' with a stout boy as the soldier! I felt extraordinarily shy and self-conscious, yet thrilled at the idea of asking a boy to 'marry me'... little aware of what that might lead to.

Before moving on, I would like to walk you through my memory of one of the school picnics, where we sat under large pine trees, singing and playing fun games. However, the song that left its imprint upon my innermost being was... '*nanha munna rahi*', which meant 'I am a small traveller, yet I am the soldier of my country'. It went on to say, 'I will walk bravely on even if I have to live with a great many difficulties. I will only relax once I have reached my destination, until then, I will go on and on, no matter what, or how many obstacles come in my way', adding, 'wherever I might toil in the hot sun; there will spring great green fields full of crops'.

These playful experiences have inspired me through my countless challenges, because I genuinely believed and practised all I learnt throughout my life.

However, soon after we had to leave Simla for good as my father's office had moved to Delhi. All of us moved into the family home at Patel Nagar and I was admitted into a school nearby. Here, I made friends with a girl called Sheryl and busied myself learning rhymes and collaborating in mischief and receiving punishments. One punishment I particularly remember was having my lips sealed with sticky tape for being noisy in the class.

There was much hustle and bustle in Delhi, and it felt strange after the peace of the hill station. Besides, I saw much less of my parents because I spent my mornings at school; Daddy had longer working, hours and Mummy was much too busy with the household chores. One afternoon, Mummy did not come to pick me up after school, and instead, my aunt was there. Hearing from her of my mother 'not feeling too well', my heart sank with fear, as I had never known or experienced an occasion when she did not come to pick me up after school. Reaching home, I raced upstairs to where I knew she would be, and my heart sank further when I saw Daddy home as well. A boiling pot of water had severely burnt her leg. Sadness and anger convulsed me like never before. This incident confirmed that Delhi was not a good place, after all. Ever so often, I would see something that caused Mummy to cry, and in addition, grandmother was always angry about one thing or another. Shrinking into a shell of fear and uncertainty, my dreams threatened to get crushed in this unpleasant atmosphere, until that is, out of the blue, there was news of our moving to Agartala in Tripura state. We would be taking all our things, except the very bulky furniture; we would travel first by train to Calcutta (now Kolkata) and thereafter by air. Wow, it all sounded fantastically exciting… my falling spirits soared once more.

I don't have much recollection about the actual journey to Calcutta, but I do remember walking around the crowded streets of the city, going to visit some distant relatives and also accompanying my parents to buy a refrigerator, which would be delivered to us at our new home in Agartala. My mother's brother and sister-in-law, Uncle Surjeet and Aunty Frauke, lived in Calcutta at that time, and we stayed with them for a few days before we caught the flight to our destination.

My uncle and aunt lived in a pretty flat in Alipur, one of Calcutta's elite colonies. Uncle Surjeet had married a German lady and had moved to India to be close to the family here. I had taken an instant liking to Aunty Frauke when I first met her at my maternal grandparents' home. Her mystic yet warm personality had instantly won my heart, and now that I was in Calcutta, I happily followed her around constantly, but felt utterly tongue-tied and shy in her presence.

Though I don't have many memories of this visit, I do remember the occasion when I watched with a watering mouth, Aunty Frauke taking the tender flesh of a chicken she had boiled off the bones and add it to the simmering white sauce I so enjoyed. I loved almost everything she cooked: chicken in white sauce along with fresh cucumbers, onion, and tomato salad laced with yummy French dressing. I did not like the mashed potatoes then, which accompanied them, though now I do.

So it was that one fateful day at the dinner table when I dared to say that I did not want the potatoes. Aunty Frauke said to me: 'Children never "want" anything,' she said firmly, 'they always must "like" or "not like" something.' Her words were engraved in my heart, and were diligently practised, till strangely one day, many years later, it was she who taught me to adhere to my inner voice. This was about nearly twenty-eight years from that day in her home, and as there is much to relate before that, I will leave it for later in this narrative.

Returning to the dinner table on the chicken-and-white-sauce evening, I vividly remember merrily polishing off everything on my plate, except the mashed potatoes. Watching me indifferently toying with the leftover heap of mashed potatoes on my plate, Aunty Frauke said, 'Come on Penny, let's help those potatoes go into your tummy,' and taking the fork from my fingers, she flattened the mound of potatoes into a large patty, which she then cut into four little triangles with her knife. 'Now, let's play *ina mina mina mo* with the four islands and you will eat up the one that gets the "mo,"' she played on, and then continuing her play, 'Oh Penny! Here, this one is left,' she laughed, 'and now this one! And now this poor one is lonely, you must get it to be with its friends inside your tummy,' she coaxed... and before I knew it, there was no potato heap for me to feel unhappy about! Once I had mastered the technique, I used it each time I felt the need to convey food I did not like from my plate into my tummy!

With these two lessons tucked away inside my head, I lose the trail of events till I see myself in Agartala, being driven in a jeep alongside my parents and brother, to take a look at Koonjabun, the housing colony, and the house which we were to occupy. It was almost dark when we arrived there. The house was surrounded by an overgrown and shabby garden with a broken bamboo fence around it. I remember walking around the then spooky looking house, but did not venture indoors as for the time being, there was no electricity.

Clearly embossed on the canvas of my memory of this maiden visit to our new home are the black blotches of giant trees against a dimly-lit evening sky. Lucid as crystal are the unfamiliar sounds of creatures of the night, filling the air with a sense of thrill and mystery. Hazy is the recollection of a stranger escorting us, but vivid are the fearsome stories he related of the abundance of snakes and dangerous lizards, called Geckos, that were to abide with us in this beautiful land where we were to spend almost four eventful years.

We moved into Number 5, Type 5 bungalow in Koonjabun, and soon settled into our new routine. In a matter of a few days, the unpacking was done, new furniture was bought, and a suitable school was located. It all seemed like a breathtaking dream. Oh, as I sit at my desk writing about those times, I can't resist letting you peep into the soaring flames of excitement raging in my heart at the mere prospect of being able to relive those wonderful moments. This acute excitement had completely erased the gloom of the suffocating Delhi experiences.

New people, new friends, remarkable customs, and a brand new language, all in one swoop. I was completely swept away! It was all very exciting. Little Sandy and I had a bedroom to ourselves with separate beds fitted with independent mosquito nets, plus an exclusive cupboard and an attached bathroom too. It was fantastic... in the middle of the night, I went to my very own washroom independently, just as grown-ups did.

My secret wish of independently communicating with friends was also magically fulfilled. Pick up the receiver, announce your desired number to the monotonous voice asking for it, and you were off chatting in seconds to the person of your choice and that too without the assistance of elders.

It was ever so exciting, that is, until one night, on one of my freedom filled bathroom trips, a huge cockroach took a fancy of planting itself onto my big toe! As soon as I stepped behind the bathroom door I felt some strange soft needles clamp on to my big toe. Unable to see what it was, panic-stricken, 'snake... gecko... God only knows what' I imagined! Shrieking wildly, I bolted from the bathroom, running as fast as my legs could carry me, and through my parents' bedroom, I flew into the drawing room... kicking my inhabited foot with vigorous jerks to dislodge the fierce rider from my toe! My passenger too seemed in shock at the sudden flight, to which it was subjected and so clung on for its dear life. After coping with a great deal of flinging and kicking, it released its hold and fell on to the settee, where it breathed its last after receiving a blow from my father. Post this encounter, I dared not venture on my big girl spree alone: I would call for Daddy, and he always scanned the net, the floor, and the bathroom before I cautiously tiptoed to the washroom.

Shortly, both Sandy and I were admitted to Shishu Bihar School, one of the very few English-medium schools here, and fortunately Bengali was taught as the second language, but non-Bengali students were exempted from the compulsion of studying it. We therefore never learnt to read or write this beautiful language, but soon mastered the spoken dialect. Besides, as most teachers in our school usually resorted to teaching in Bengali, I became fluent in the language, and how fortunate that proved later, at an appropriate time in this narrative, you will discover why I say this.

Although Sandy and I went to the same school, we had an hour's difference in our timings. The bus stop was about a two-minute walk from our house. As Sandy was very young, he was accompanied to the bus stop by Mummy or Daddy, while I walked down with my schoolmates from the neighbourhood. On days when my friends were not going, my parents accompanied me.

On one such morning, Daddy introduced me to the magnificent Red Silk Cotton tree, growing near my bus stop. He picked up one of the large flowers and handed it to me. Fascinated by the tough outer green cup-like structure, clasping the crimson velvety petals and the long slender pollen stems, I clutched the contraption close to my cheek! Intrigued by its softness, I slid my finger along the petals, imagining the thrill of the bees and butterflies, landing on it in comfort, gliding gleefully to drink the sweet nectar within. By then, my quest to see the flower in its entirety had come alive and I sniffed the beauty for its fragrance and attempted to stick my tongue in to partake of the sweet liquid that must lie within! You see, I have always been greatly interested in observing things in extreme detail, and have intensively utilized all my available tools: my sight, my nose, ears, mouth, and sensation to obtain the best results. The hooting of my school-bus horn brought me out of my flower land and still wrapped in my dream, away I drove off in the rickety black bus.

Shishu Bihar School was situated in the heart of the town, separated from our newly developing residential area by a narrow rainwater stream. The pungent smell of rotting fish indicated the arrival of school, and up surged the horrible sinking sensation inside my stomach. It stemmed from the daily ordeal of dismounting the school bus and conveying my belongings safely to my classroom. Trembling with inexplicable fear, clutching my school bag and water bottle tightly, I would almost tumble from the three precariously suspended steps of the bus. Then with the bright sunlight virtually blinding me, I would place one foot in front of the other, with only the sounds of other children defining the direction I must take!

I silently endured this horror, terrified at every step I took treading into the unseen, my tiny heart constantly thumping against my ribs. Even so, the thought of sharing my fears or staying away from school never occurred to me, probably because I saw no other child around me create a fuss about getting off the bus and walking to class. Instead, I endured this daily ordeal, thinking about the secrets that would unfold from between my books, the fascinating stories the lessons would reveal, the ramblings around the compound, the fun that I would have chattering and playing once I was through with this treacherous journey!

Our school was housed in a single-storey rectangular building with a slanting roof and a large courtyard in the centre. The headmistress's office and kindergarten classes occupied the front of the building and the senior classes were held in the rear wing. Rain trees, mango, and jackfruit trees spread their ever-green shade over the school building, and massive bougainvillea and hibiscus plants created a natural boundary around the grounds. There were not more than about fifteen children a class and the sixth grade, the senior-most class in the school, had only six students.

Miss Patro (the headmistress) was a severe looking middle-aged spinster who everyone feared. No matter what she looked like, I think she was after all a wise old lady because she provided us with a host of extra-curricular activities together with the mandatory study curriculum within the strict bounds of discipline. She, however, certainly had a thing about 'no exposure'... the length of our dresses had to reach three inches below our knees, or else...!

Well, in the ultimate analysis, I loved school and must have been a very attentive student because I don't recall doing much homework. Actually, after we returned from school, on most afternoons, I, together with my friend, Madhumita Pal from next door, slipped away into our back garden, to scramble up the muddy hillock at the side of the garden on to the giant jackfruit tree. Concealed amongst the dark green leaves of the massive tree, we enjoyed in seclusion oranges and bits of tamarind we managed to smuggle up with us. Madhu, as I called her, would every afternoon inevitably have a new ghost story to narrate, providing thrill and mystery to our afternoon expedition. These mystical moments were also utilized to plan the official, evening playtime activities.

Our tree meeting was usually terminated by the commencement of a daughter hunt by one of our mothers, and now that I have first hand experience of motherhood, I realize that it was never a secret after all. Anyhow, we would then coyly troop indoors and were coaxed into taking a forced siesta. Sandy and my mother did manage a nap or two, but I was forever too restless on my side of the bed to shut my eyes for even a moment. Thus, on most afternoons, wretched with uselessly tossing and turning in bed, I often crept out barefoot into the back veranda through the wooden mesh door, and potter around the garden, tiptoeing in between into the kitchen for a tasty snack.

On one such wondrous afternoon excursion, I had suspended myself on to the kitchen shelf to reach for the sugar for my hush-hush sweet anise-seed paste recipe, and it taught me one of life's important lessons. Well, it happened that the sugar jar in hand, dreaming of the tasty concoction I was about to create, I jumped on to the kitchen floor expecting to land soundlessly on to the meticulously clean cement surface. Instead, a large scaly, balloon-like object ejaculating a sticky liquid leapt on my bare foot. My heart stopped, and panic-stricken I shrieked and my guilty secret was revealed too. The attacker was my good old friend, the cockroach. To this day, the mere touch of anything other than the floor or my footwear makes my blood run cold! Happily for my mother, never again did I ramble without footwear... a small price it may sound to have your kids wearing their slippers. However that may be, it wasn't much fun to have cockroaches playing the role of shock-absorbers for jumping feet!

Other than these trifling incidents, life darted along, frisking and frolicking like a stream flowing through green meadows under the crystal blue sky; joy, love, and freedom was all mine. I feared nothing but the crazy insects which were kept skillfully at bay by my wonderful parents and maid; or the short, independent walks that were the product of necessity. My days were so utterly packed with exciting happenings that the terror of walking around alone was thrust into oblivion. I was too preoccupied, racing around playing hopscotch, or hide-and-seek, milling about the wonders of nature, and travelling to new places to worry about the fear of walking to class without holding someone's hand. So long I did everything my friends did, I didn't worry about having to be the first one out during a game of catching catch or the den while playing hide-and-seek. Besides, in any event, I always won at playing dark room, and was more confident in the dark than any of my friends.

Daddy too was busy with his work, while Mummy was occupied with the care of both us children and our home. They always were smiling and cheerful, radiating a complete sense of security which provided us with a comfortable and relaxed atmosphere.

Sandy was fast growing up and proving to be an active boy who loved the outdoors and would regularly come home with cuts and bruises, dust stained in the course of fearless outings. I sometimes really admired his skill with the first-aid box, because I, by contrast, was the complete opposite; if by chance I did manage to cut myself and blood sneaked out, I wailed and fretted for hours on end.

You can therefore very well imagine my plight when one evening I found myself walking along with my parents into Dr D.R. Nandi's clinic. I remember that soon thereafter, I was quaking with fear as I lay on the examination table in a dingy room undergoing a medical exam. Dr Nandi spoke gently to me while he held the stethoscope to my chest, poked my tummy, pricked needles into me, and even knocked away at my bones with something so hard that it felt almost like a hammer. My amazement at the sudden visit to the doctor had left me distressed and shaken.

At the conclusion of the medical exam, I was led into the adjoining room to wait for my parents who were in the doctor's consulting room. I sat alone in the drab waiting room, my spirits dampened, and my habitual sunny smile banished behind a cloud of unknown worry. My head swam with gloomy thoughts; just when I was so happy and everything was going on fine, why did they have to bring me here? What on earth are they going to do with me next? Will they cut me up to look inside me or will they give me injections and bitter medicines?

The sound of a door opening roused me from my mournful thoughts, and the soothing voices of Mummy and Daddy lifted up my falling spirits. After all, I thought gratefully, I seem to be escaping from the doctor's visit perfectly unscathed.

Relieved and happy at my escape, I hastened to tuck myself away into the rear seat of our Fiat. On the drive home, I heard the great news of an indefinite holiday with my favourite aunty in Calcutta, and in an instant, the ordeal of the visit to the doctor vanished. The thrill of being with my Aunty Frauke, plus another airplane ride, revived my sagging spirits.

The very next morning, the four of us, the fourth not daddy, but dear little Cathy, my beloved talking freckled-nosed doll, with long black hair went. She had come to be my little baby, gifted to me by Mr H.C. Lark, an American acquaintance of my father.

Mummy sat little Sandy on her knees in the aircraft, while I cleverly seated Cathy on the service table in front of me. The airhostesses were enchanted with my little doll and offered to give me extra sweets for my tiny charge. Apparently, Cathy had made me the centre of attraction on the plane. I loved it. It made me feel important as I carried Cathy around with an enhanced sense of pride.

Cradling my doll in one arm, holding Mummy's hand with the other, I alighted from the plane to be met by a tall blue-eyed blond fairy: my aunt! Taking my hand into hers as she chatted with Mummy, Aunty Frauke briskly led us to her car. I sat snuggling shyly close to her, breathing in her soft, yet heady perfume, as our car weaved its way through the heavy traffic and came to stop in the parking lot of a very large building. Stepping out of the car, still clutching Cathy close, I followed the two ladies up the beautiful wide marble stairway which led to Aunty Frauke's home. I had never seen such a magnificent structure. Wide-eyed and bursting with curiosity, yet too shy to express my awe, I quietly walked along.

There were three white doors on the first floor and I wished we were entering the one with a golden ring hanging on it, and lo and behold, that very door was opened for us. My wish had come true again, and we entered a luxuriously furnished and tastefully decorated flat.

Sunlight streaming in through the large bay window, framed by the dark gray of the walls and with delicate white net curtains lent extreme elegance to the sitting room. It was spotlessly clean, like a little palace out of a storybook. Approaching us, from the other end of the large sitting-cum dining room, appeared a grinning man all dressed in white, carrying a tray laden with cool lemonade and yummy smelling biscuits. This man was no other than the fantastic cook whose craft was to regale us through the months ahead.

Our bedroom too was a comfortable, medium-sized room with built-in cupboards, soft springy beds, and a cute little attached bathroom complete with a fancy tub lending a touch of luxury to the setting. It was a true fairyland with a real fairy in the garb of my beautiful aunt. Yet, a shadow always seemed to lurk in the back of my mind. This silhouette was the mysterious fear of my uncle, and the cause remains a mystery to this day. The truth is that Uncle Surjeet has always been a generous person, bringing us presents and taking us out whenever there was an occasion for us to be together, yet, from the moment I first met him, I have invariably been nervous in his presence. This has indeed been an open secret and sometimes even a joke within the family.

Uncle Surjeet worked with the General Electrical Company (GEC) and Aunty Frauke, at the German Consulate. Engulfed by their warm hospitality, we seamlessly settled into their home, and set about the business that had brought us here. From the next day onward, Mummy and the two of us trudged from eye clinic to eye hospital, hoping to find a remedy for my dreaded vision impairment.

At these clinics, I would have to undergo all kinds of strange tests and probes into my eyes and head. Without mercy, countless drops of atropine were forced into my eyes, ignoring the loud protests I emitted. No matter how much I cried or pleaded, nothing seemed to release me from painful injections and petrifying examinations. It took all my self-control to refrain from the powerful urge to strike the doctors while they breathed into my face, shining dazzling lights into my eyes!

It became a never-ending trauma, of trial frames being constantly slipped on to my nose and various trial glasses unsuccessfully tried on. Thereafter, I was repeatedly asked for my opinion on the clarity of these ridiculous little things, to which I unswervingly gave negative answers. By then I had overheard the alarming possibility of being made to wear spectacles, which was totally unacceptable to me. I therefore decided to do whatever it took to keep the horrible things out of my life. Thereafter, without giving it a second thought, no matter what, I made certain with all my might that I would never wear spectacles... and I never did!

To achieve my goal of avoiding spectacles at all costs, I went as far as trying to misguide the doctors by cooking up dialogues like, 'This one has made everything cloudy; and with this one, I can't see anything at all'. Of course, now that I reflect upon this episode, I can honestly say that none of the trial glasses made much of an improvement in my vision anyway, yet a few lenses did make the letters on the vision chart appear bigger and closer. I had however, of course made up my mind, and nothing in the world would change it. However, in the years that followed, there have been times when I longed to see with my eyes and wished there had been a way I could have been helped by the miracle of spectacles. At the time, however, little did I know what I was asking for; I went as far as praying anxiously to God: 'Oh dear God, please let them not find any spectacles for me; please, never in my life should I be able to use any of these horrible attachments.' Also, each time the decision went in my favour, of 'Sorry, no spectacles seem to help', I was overjoyed and thanked God for granting my wish!

Back home from these treacherous trips to the medical tyrants, I lost no time or energy in soaking up the fun and pleasure, which went hand in hand with our unique and out of the blue Calcutta tour. There were so many fascinating activities to be undertaken as soon as we got home that I instantaneously shed my agony. Nothing could dampen the thrill I got from prowling around cars parked in the parking lot downstairs, sneaking up dingy staircases or peering at the beautiful coloured pictures in books and magazines that lay on the majestic sideboard in the drawing room.

On days when there were electricity cuts, my aunt took us all to splash away the heat at the Calcutta Swimming Club. The big pools frightened me, so I was content to wade in the round baby pool with a large gushing fountain-like waterfall in its midst, and an occasional ride on my aunt's back around the big pool. Little Sandy was, however, a shade too eager to fling himself into the big pool and it proved quite a struggle to keep him away. I would be quite nervous for his dear life and kept calling for him, but well, barring a few heart-stopping incidents of people fishing him out of the water, we had, to say the least, a wonderful time.

Our first 'treatment' trip to Calcutta lasted three months, and was followed by many more. On one of these trips, I accompanied my mother and Aunty Frauke to watch the first motion picture of my life in a cinema hall. The Globe cinema hall in the heart of Calcutta, and I was to watch *The Sound of Music.*

Forgive me if I take a few moments to dwell on this entrancing experience. We walked into a massive darkened hall full of chairs, sat on comfortable seats, along with a great many people. We had probably arrived just in the nick of time as the film started immediately, and therefore I can only recount from the shelves of memory my sitting and gazing mesmerized at the great silver screen ahead.

I was virtually transported, body and soul into the film, and became one with the vast blue sky, the lofty green mountains, sailing on the cool clear breeze, feeling as though this world was a part of me. Oh, what a magnificent world lay there before me to enjoy and to claim. My head swam with the sound of music and then, as Maria jumped off the tree into the grounds of the church, speeding in from her ramblings on the hills, I became her in totality. From then on, I spoke every word she did, I sang every song she sang, and I felt every emotion she felt... I deliberately began thinking and almost literally acting like her... now Maria's character was transfixed upon my own forever. This film merits special mention in this narrative because of the important role it played in shaping my personality and romantic dreams.

Before continuing to paint my life's canvas, I would like to mention some more of the incredible efforts nature made to prepare me for the disability I was to live with. Many idle evenings at my aunt's home were spent listening to stories read to me, and the one of Helen Keller truly fascinated me. I was deeply moved by the harshness of her multiple disabilities and greatly admired the heights to which she rose. I have very often drawn inspiration from the fact that if she could achieve so much with three out of her five senses impaired, what stopped me from doing the same with four of mine perfectly intact?

Thereafter, following innumerable visits to Calcutta for in-depth consultancy with the most competent doctors, it was revealed that both the optic nerves of my eyes were, for reasons unknown, partially paralyzed. We sadly accepted the final verdict that no treatment anywhere in the world was available for this condition.

Thus, much disappointed, I was happy to return to the day-to-day routine I had left behind ever so abruptly. Little did I know that life was never going to be the same again, everything had changed! Friends, teachers, and neighbours, all looked at me with pity; I seemed to have been transformed into a strange pitiful object to be handled with extra consideration or simply left alone!

I was completely taken aback by this attitude. According to me, I was the same girl who had gone off to Calcutta while everyone else went to school. What was it that had altered here while I was away? Here I was back, all excited, eager to share all the wonderful experiences I came loaded with from the big bustling city, and to my dismay, no one seemed to be interested in what I had brought back.

Puzzled and confused, I kept searching for an answer to this inexplicable question. How was I to live a dull and sad life, and that too without my friends and everyone else I was so fond of? I was completely bewildered and felt guilty for some unknown crime I had committed. I even wondered whether it had been wrong on my part to have strayed off on such a long holiday, while everyone else went to school. Could that have been the reason for all the unexpected behaviour I was being subjected to? I wondered why I felt like crying all the time. Was something the matter with me? Why did my friends now never come to call me to join them at playtime? Occasionally, when out of sheer desperation to be out there with them, I managed to gather the courage to go out myself to join them, why did they have to manufacture excuses to somehow send me back home? Yes, the only people that had not changed were my lovely parents and little Sandy! And how happy was I for this one blessing.

I had certainly not opted willingly to face multiple challenges, like losing my eyesight plus my right to be like everyone else, and that too all of a sudden. However that might be, now that I was in a fix, and a terrible one at that, I had to do something about it. 'Life couldn't go on like this,' I must have declared to myself. 'Never mind what they all make me feel, I just can't just sit around sulking and depressed, waiting for life to get back to normal, when nothing at all is wrong with me.' I therefore decided to carry on living life, ignoring at all costs, the attitude that surrounded me, convinced that things would automatically fall back into place. I pushed my tears and sadness aside, and flung myself into the usual timetable of life. Whenever I felt like crying, I would try to hide and weep a bit on my own, and then the thought of depressing my parents with my tears caused me to hastily wipe them away.

Slowly but surely, I began to resume my lost position in my little world, and when I was just about edging my way along with my heavy load, the terror struck afresh! This time, the villain of the piece was a smallpox vaccine.

It was inoculation time in the summer of 1967; our school had a visiting doctor to administer the smallpox and TABC shots to all the students. I recall walking along with other children to the hall and holding out a trembling arm in front of the doctor, dreading the anticipated attack of the needle upon it. It was all over and done within an instant and after all, was not half as bad as I had imagined.

Well, with a sigh of relief I walked back to my classroom quite unharmed and peered at the two tiny reddish spots that appeared upon the tender skin of the inside of my lower arm. These dots fortunately seemed to give no pain, so I swept aside the worry and returned to the events of the day.

The following morning, I had a swollen and painful arm as well as a little fever. I was happy to learn that I would be up and running in a day or so, as the after-effect of this injection was relatively brief. This assurance provided only brief satisfaction, as the two red dots of the smallpox vaccine began looking and feeling worse with each passing moment. In the days that passed, they turned into two dark brown marbles sticking out from a bed of swollen and painful angry rashes upon my arm. Off I was taken to the skin specialist to have my new ailment attended to. The number of pills I had to swallow increased, and all kinds of horrid smelling ointments were applied to my arm, making it look even more unsightly.

I had to keep the wound exposed for it to heal quickly, and it certainly presented a ghastly sight. No one wanted to have me around, and some of my friends went as far as breaking their friendship with me because they did not wish to contract my disease. My mother's repeated attempts to convince my friends of the non-infectious nature of my skin disorder too proved unsuccessful. Anyhow, I was inwardly quite content to be left alone because I myself was most self-conscious and uncomfortable with my condition and felt more comfortable indoors.

So tragically imprisoned and deeply saddened, I spent most of my time alone, feeling like a bird that had lost its wings and yet could not abandon a longing to fly. Discomfort, pain, shame, and unfathomable loneliness engulfed my heart. My magical gift to bounce back in the face of adversity had simply given me the slip on this onset of hardship, and I was utterly crushed.

Downcast and listless, I went about my monotonous existence with no particular quest, awaiting release from this painful skin disorder. After what seemed ages, the day arrived when my rash disappeared from my arm and I returned to join the flurry of everyday life.

Oddly, however, my companions appeared to have forgotten my ugly disease and had ceased their hostility towards me; I, for my part, had fallen into a peculiar sense of contemplation. While my relish for life had wholly returned, the happenings of the past months had imprinted on my heart and soul, an unidentifiable set of astringent realities. Gradually over the years, I was able to decode these impressions when advancing age and experience provided me with the necessary tools for this.

Well, before I move on towards other significant events relating to my growing-up years, I would like to mention that this skin disorder stayed with me for the next forty years... waxing and waning, appearing in various forms and intensities over the years. There were often very long periods when I was bedridden as a consequence of severely infected and painful sores, sometimes for as long as six months at a stretch, as handicapped and dependent on others for such trifles as eating my food and using the washroom!

This proved to be the most disabling element in my life as it deprived me of a great many opportunities besides hurting my self-esteem with its ugliness and the discomfort it imposed.

As life has its way of moving on and events have theirs of periodically occurring carried along through them in my unique splashing and swirling fashion... riding a wave here and hitting a rock there... I moved on.

We remained in Agartala for four long years, and even though two of my life-shattering tribulations struck in this land of pineapples and jackfruits, I have very fond memories of it, which overall dilute the immeasurable suffering I endured there.

On days I felt well, I would be out playing cricket with friends. We played on the road outside our home and used a dining chair in place of wickets and a permanent team member was positioned to hastily drag it out of the middle of the road if a vehicle dared to pass that way. Also, as I was not a very good fielder, I was almost always assigned the task of chair attendant, at which I was superb: car approached, and away I dragged the 'chair-wicket' at top speed to the edge of the road... danger departed... back I hauled the mobile wicket.

Though my batting gave my team very little pleasure as it was a very rare occasion indeed when the ball happened to touch my bat and a run or two were added to our score, there were many others who were even less successful. As there were certain little players who ran off the batting pitch at the mere suspicion of a dog in the vicinity. Besides, I was well aware that few can be good at everything and anyhow, I was too overjoyed to be amongst friends to bother about things in which I performed poorly.

Then there would come the picnic fever, and we would abandon ourselves wholeheartedly to the desire to eat and drink, sing and gossip in an uninhabited territory. To these picnics, we carried home-made sandwiches and cakes with freshly-cut pineapples and peanuts, packed into baskets, to the back gardens of deserted houses or to some other secluded spot where we were certain that grown-ups would not intrude. We once tried our hand at cooking in the open, and the breathtaking excitement of a real fire and proper cooking vessels, peeling real potatoes with real knives, and using all the ingredients that big people did was extremely exhilarating.

Also unforgettable are the periods spent at school: all subjects seemed to go straight from the teacher's mouth into my head. I did some written class-work in a scribble, but thoroughly absorbed all my lessons, drawing on the canvas of my memory every concept my teachers taught verbally. Conducting science experiments was sheer joy, and arithmetic classes were ever so challenging.

During those days in Agartala, my mother did all her stitching herself and had a flair and passion for embroidery. She took great pride in the pansies and daisies she created on bedspreads and cushion covers, and her handiwork were greatly admired. This intricate skill caught my fancy and I was keen to follow suit. You will wonder how I was able to see what Mummy was producing. Well, although I was exceedingly short-sighted, I could still observe most reasonable sized objects quite clearly, provided I held them almost next to my eyes, which I unfailingly did. I therefore revealed my yearning to learn this delicate art, and my sweet mother promptly agreed, and never allowed me even to sense that I would never be able to manage the needlework given my failing eyesight. She once again allowed me to define my own limits; to discover for myself the extent of my ability and with an encouraging 'Very well, my dear', went along to get the material necessary for my embroidery classes.

I was soon the proud owner of my very own embroidery frame, a slightly fat needle, and a bunch of colourful embroidery thread. Then with her black eyebrow pencil, my mother drew the pattern of a large flower, taking care to draw very dark thick outlines, on my material. Then, threading the fat needle with a gorgeous red thread, she gave it to me, and holding my hand in hers, showed me what I should do.

In great earnest, I stuck the apparatus very close to my face so that I could see something of the drawing on the frame, and eagerly set to work, following the instruction with the utmost precision and getting the needle in and out of the cloth... hoping to witness at least one red-coloured petal at the end of my labour. Subsequent to great struggle and concentration, I remember taking a look at my handiwork, and, from the embroidery frame, gazed at an untidy red blotch!

The red flower turning into a red blotch was terribly distressing, disheartening, and altogether unacceptable; the frustration and sense of defeat made me cry endlessly. 'Why is yours so good and mine so untidy?' I cried. 'I worked so hard... then why does it look so ugly?' Seeing me so deeply afflicted, my mother secretly put away our embroidery and instead pulled out her knitting needles.

Once again, I was after her to teach me to knit; and this time, she had done just the right thing. I knitted my darling Cathy her first bright yellow pullover. After this, I knitted a black muffler too, but invariably wondered how certain mysterious holes appeared in my knitting! By and by, I discovered that the holes were the stitches I dropped off the knitting needles. I therefore pulled it apart and re-knitted it over and over again until I achieved the high standards set by my mother's knitting. My knitting needles have ever since been my best friends.

Oh, and last but not the least, I must mention my dancing lessons and our queer dance master. We had dancing classes twice a week, where our mischievous gang spent more time tricking the poor simple soul, instead of learning the art. Oh, we did wish to learn dancing, but there was so much else to be done during the day that ever so often, we had to get out of the organized dance class to attend to these important little businesses!

Various innovative methods of dodging the dance master would be crafted, but he did eventually succeed in teaching us a lot of Indian classical dance! So much so, that each year during the festive season, he got us to perform on stage, and there, I was in my element.

The exuberance of riding bicycles and splashing fabric paints on handkerchiefs, attending birthday parties, and going to the gurdwara in the army campus was just wonderful.

Then, once again, my father's job profile, presented us with the opportunity to travel by road through the eastern Indian states. And as travel has always been another of my 'favourite things', I will take you down that particular memory lane too!

Well, so it was my days in Agartala sped, laughing and crying, singing and dancing, picnicking and conspiring to my heart's content. Normally, we went up north to visit relatives during our vacations, but a few holidays were spent touring the neighbouring north-eastern states.

Our first such tour took us to visit my father's cousin, Aruna, and her husband Arjun Malhotra, at the tea gardens near Silchar, and what a holiday that proved to be! The nostalgia of their magnificent home and sprawling estate lingers on in my mind. As we alighted from the jeep, I walked awestruck through the expansive lush green sloping lawns towards the wide steps leading to the homestead surrounded by a mesh-covered verandah rising against the glittering blue of the afternoon sky!

As I stepped indoors, the overwhelming ambience made me feel like a tiny ant would feel inside my pencil box. After being warmly greeted by Aunty Topsy (Aruna) and Uncle Arjun, we were ushered into their grand drawing room. The rest of the day sped away listening to the elders chattering and following little Sandy running around exploring the premises, in addition to gorging on the delicious treats laid out for our welcome.

Everything went just fine until bedtime, when I discovered that both Sandy and I were to sleep together, on our own, in a separate bedroom on a big soft double bed at the centre of this huge room. 'Where will Mummy and Daddy sleep?', I enquired, as I was allotted one side of the big bed and Sandy, the other. 'Oh, they have their own bedroom next to ours, my dear,' declared Aunty Topsy cheerfully. 'Let them enjoy some undisturbed slumber while they are here, and I will look after you.' My heart sank at the thought of 'new house, new place, new room, and on top of that, no Mummy or Daddy to call out to from my bed!' I said nothing... but never had I felt so utterly helpless and frightened, yet, too proud to voice my fears, I simply braved it out through the first night and by the next night, sleeping independently seemed wonderful! Sure enough, on the first night with Mom and Dad far far away, I woke up and managed to figure out the way to the washroom, by feeling my way to the bedroom wall nearest to my bed and following it till I got there.

With my courage and confidence enhanced by the past night's experience, I soon learnt my way around the house and the fabulous garden. It proved to be a truly enthralling holiday, filled with visits to the tea gardens, the tea factory, elephant rides, and expeditions into the wilderness.

The ecstasy of the cruise down the river Eijol in a primitive boat through a thickly forested valley still remains fresh in my memory. Our precarious climb up the steep bank, a tribal village perched at the top, tiny bamboo huts built there out of long bamboo stems, made a pretty sight. Children running around naked, babies sleeping in hammocks swinging from the thatched roofs of the huts perched aloft while topless women and men clad in colourful pieces of cloth tied around their waists and bead necklaces dangling around their necks made me feel as though I was walking through a picture book.

We clambered to one of these huts perched aloft via a precarious step-ladder contrived out of a single piece of bamboo slashed in places to provide footholds. Inside were women suckling their tiny babies, who, when we arrived, immediately brought out some home-brewed rice wine in vessels made of dried pumpkin shells and served it in baked mud tumblers. Of course I was not to taste any, as I was much too young for intoxicating brews.

Our second trip into the north-east was undertaken in the car of the district magistrate, Mr S.M. Kanver, along with his girlfriend, who joined us in Silchar. We set out from Agartala, driving first to Silchar and then going on to Shillong, and then on to Siliguri, Darjeeling, Kalingpong, right up to Gangtok in Sikkim. We stopped over at the Kaziranga game sanctuary for a couple of days and rode out into the forest on elephant back to make the acquaintance of the majestic rhinoceros and wild buffalos there. We stayed at the pretty double-storied forest bungalow at the edge of the jungle, and there the skull of a real elephant lay in the garden. At this guesthouse to simply satisfy my curiosity, I even tried reaching over into a bird's nest from where I heard little baby birds squeaking, in the process, nearly toppling off the service ladder.

This too was an unforgettable trip, laden with never-to-be-erased impressions engraved on my mind. Once again, I am obliged to confess the reality of having been granted a golden opportunity of capturing forever the phenomenal bounty of the world, with the somewhat dysfunctional camera of my sight. Now, stored away in the depths of memory are vivid pictures of countless intriguing shapes and colours of insects and birds, glorious landscapes, and fantastic man-made wonders I gathered in those distant days.

Returning from the holidays was almost as exciting an event for me as setting out was. There was so much I had gathered during the twenty-one days away from school which I was almost impatient to spill out to eager listeners. Then of course, there was usually the element of being able to show off the trinkets I had collected from the places to which I had gone, and as you must have guessed by now, I reveled on the abundant attention I received as one possessing things others hadn't got.

Our return journey commenced aboard the miniature toy train from Darjeeling to Siliguri and then by a bigger one to Dharamnagar in Tripura state. From there, we were to travel by road to Agartala, as the car with the rest of the party was to go on to Delhi. The ride on the toy train was amazing, and as the name suggests, this train actually looks like a toy running almost all the time alongside the winding steep road; you can very easily jump off the running locomotive, pick your favourite flowers, and jump back into your carriage at the next bend in the mountain. Of course, I dared not jump off, but the leisurely twisting and turning of the little caterpillar train provided me with the opportunity to take in the beauty of the hills, which too became a part of the collection on the shelves of my memory closet.

Following the entrancing journey down the eastern Himalayan range, sitting in another train gliding along the emerald paddy-fields of Assam, I witnessed another heart-rending sight, which left me shaken. Just as the gray dusk was melting into darkness, our train came to a halt at a small station. Dinner was loaded on to the train, and as soon as it rolled into motion again, large steel dishes piled high with rice, vegetables, and dal, was served to passengers. In about an hour, the train once again stopped, and in an instant, the carriages were raided by hordes of little children hauling empty cane baskets behind them.

The little kids shoved their way through the passengers, and grabbed with astonishing swiftness the used dinner dishes, and then, with immense alacrity, emptied the leftover food into their little baskets.

Horror-struck at the sight, I wondered what this all meant. Gradually, it dawned on me that they were here to gather the leftover food. This was the appalling necessity that poverty enforced upon the innocent little inhabitants of this region, who kept themselves alive by consuming the leftovers of travellers on the few trains that passed by. The profound impression of this episode laid the foundation of my belief in later life to count my blessings.

Thus, filled with a bundle of sweet and bitter experiences, my second vacation to the north-east came to an end.

Back home, time skipped past. Mornings spent at school, afternoons whirled by playing, and the evenings were spent with the family. Visitors came and went, picnics and parties had me swinging, and amidst all this, my disability was completely forgotten! My skin disorder kept bouncing in and out of my days, putting me out of sorts while it raged, but I learnt to swiftly bounce back the moment it subsided. Now, before I move away from the tales of my travels, I would like to tell you about just one more intriguing tour.

It was summer holiday time again, and my heart was nearly bursting with the excitement that lay ahead. We were to go via Calcutta to Delhi, to spend a few days with our relatives there and then move on to visit my maternal grandparents, who were, at that time, in Kashmir, the paradise of the world.

As usual, we took a flight from Agartala to Calcutta and undertook the rest of the journey by train up to Pathankot in the foothills. From there, we were to travel through the northern Himalaya, and lodged luxuriously at the back of a police truck.

The twining and twisting roads on the lush green Himalayan ranges, and the cool clean wind blowing in my face had me spellbound. We were faced with the prospect of spending the night en route at a dingy looking primitive roadside teahouse inn. The rooms here were so spooky and filthy that my parents decided that we should instead sleep in the back of the truck. Mattresses were pulled out of the bedrolls and spread on the floor of the truck and the sides covered with tarpaulin to form an instant roadside bedroom.

I awoke the following morning in a swaying and bumpy bed, to delightedly discover that we had resumed our journey early that morning. Shortly thereafter, we drove into the exquisite city of the Mughal Gardens, the famous Dal Lake, shikaras, and the 'luxurious houseboats', and giant green natural archways formed by maple and cherry trees. Presently, our caravan came to a final halt under the porch of the tourist hostel, where my grandfather's temporary quarters were located. Here, to welcome us were my grandparents along with the clear blue summer sky showering golden sunlight and the emerald green lawns lined with colourful flower beds.

We spent nearly three weeks in Kashmir and, as always, saw every nook and corner of the historic state! I went sledging on some days and very often went boating on the Dal Lake in the lovely shikaras. Going shopping fascinated me. I peered longingly at the magnificent precious and semi-precious stone jewellery and the famous papier mâché and intricately carved wood articles displayed in the glittering windows. Eventually, from those windows, a silver ring with a heart-shaped piece of jade delicately perched on it, a wooden pencil box with a carved lid, and a tiny porcelain tea set was purchased for me.

It was as though destiny was magnanimously gathering stars and tucking them away in the closet of remembrances to light up the dark and dreary path that lay ahead! I say this because, remarkably, countless adventures and experiences formed part of my childhood reality, while a fraction of my sight still lingered.

Well, it was the winter of 1969, Uncle Bhajo, Mummy's other brother, accompanied by his wife, Aunty Shirley and their four-year-old son Simon, were to visit India from Ireland. This was a major event because the family would be uniting after twenty-one years of separation. We were to spend Christmas at Uncle Surjeet's home in Calcutta where the Irish were to first land; thereafter, we were to proceed to Chandigarh to my grandparents' to spend the rest of the vacation.

Brimming with excitement, I landed at Calcutta together with my parents and Sandy, and the next thing I can remember is a house resonant with cheerful chatter and lots of presents going around! A gorgeous red handbag and beautiful pair of white denim trousers, a smart matching top, and a handful of costume jewellery had found their way into my lap too. I promptly raced off to don the new attire so I could show off my beautiful self to the visitors from Ireland, but alas the stylish trousers proved to be too tight for me. This was my first encounter with self-consciousness, triggered by the additional unsightly kilos nestling over me. Anyhow, I had to sadly forgo the trousers but had all the other gifts to cherish and enjoy.

Christmas over, we headed to Chandigarh, one of the best-planned cities in north India. At the end of a 30-hour journey, we arrived at my grandfather's house, which was a large and elegant two-storied structure, with three tall Ashoka trees lined up near the front boundary wall. Beyond it was a lush green lawn trimmed with colourful flower beds and a wide driveway on the side. Our excited group burst into the house on the first floor amidst shrieks and yells of joy, jostling about to fall into the welcoming arms of the senior most members of the family. Awaiting the arrival of the party was, along with my grandfather and step-grandmother, my grandfather's eldest sister, who was known to us all as 'Buaji'.

The celebrations of coming together were now on in earnest, overflowing with joy-filled hearts, one moment with roaring laughter and the next melting into tearful sniffs. Each one was in their own special way attempting to make up for the lost twenty-one years that had melted by. The kitchen was stuffed with special delicacies; everyone's favourite dishes were trying to find their way on to the dining table. The intense gaiety simply established the fact that for the present, the entire world had squeezed itself into this home. My father was in Delhi for some official work and was to return to Agartala from there.

Soon, the initial commotion settled down and unpacking, accompanied by a great many cups of tea and coffee, got underway. My two European aunts were very often perplexed with the extreme diversity of Indian culture. There was, in addition, the language barrier to be overcome between the two old ladies and their foreign daughters-in-law. To top it all, our cook too was beside himself with glee and awe at the opportunity of being at such close proximity with European women! Although there were an equal number of translators available, including me, major misunderstandings were being confronted. I for one was almost always, out of breath, translating and laughing all in the same time.

This was the case one morning when Aunty Shirley had taken herself into the kitchen to boil potatoes for Simon and was looking around for the wherewithal to accomplish her task when I suggested she could use a pressure cooker. Our dear cook overheard my suggestion and saw Aunty Shirley's expression brighten and in a wink, presented himself to her. She was ever so startled by this and her brightened countenance turned into a question mark. Before I could step in and sort out the confusion, the cook enthusiastically proclaimed in broken English, 'Madam', he smiled, 'I, cooker, I, cooker!' I myself was astonished at his strange and enthusiastic outburst, and so went on to ask him what he was trying to communicate. He told me bashfully that he had heard the word cooker mentioned to madam by me and understood that she was looking for him, and therefore without delay, he had presented himself! Well, there were many such incidents to sustain the fun and frolic.

Bedtime found everyone sprawled all over the three rooms for the night on a variety of contrivances. I too delightedly snuggled into Buaji's folding bed and slipped away into deep contented slumber to wake up next morning to my mother's soft joyful chatter with the elders, amidst a tinkling of teacups and the aroma of biscuits.

Lying awake, on the morning of our second day at my grandparents' home, daydreaming, I snuggled deeper under the covers, looking forward to another day of fun and amusement. The shrill ring of the doorbell brought me back into the present and I heard a messenger announce to my mother that there was a phone call for her in the house across the street. (You see, telephones at that time were a rare luxury and there were just a few phones in the neighborhood.) Mummy, appearing just a bit worried and perplexed, hurried to take the call, which she was informed was from Delhi. Papa, 'my grandfather', accompanied her and they both soon returned with the ever so upsetting news of my father's sudden illness in Delhi.

At this time, Mummy had been suffering with a sore throat, but after this call, she lost her voice completely. In less than an audible whisper, she told me, 'Perhaps you would like to stay here with your aunts and uncles and grandparents, while both Sandy and I go to Delhi to look after Daddy. He is in hospital, and Sandy is too young to manage without me,' she went on, her face assuming a tragic expression. 'We will both be back as soon as your father is better; is that OK with you dear?'

I of course agreed to this proposition. Mummy did seem worried and sad, but I was certain that illnesses came and disappeared, and Daddy would be well pretty soon. I was quite happy anyway to be able to spend time with my favourite Aunty Frauke. Moreover, I was now a big girl, and therefore was capable of taking care of myself. Apart, that is, from the task of doing up my long hair and hooking up the dress behind my back, and this too would somehow be managed.

By mid-morning therefore, Mummy and Sandy left for Delhi and I was left to my own devices to fend for myself with the rest of my extended family. Later, I discovered that Mummy would have to remain in Delhi indefinitely, as my father had suffered a major heart attack and his recovery would take time. Therefore, at the end of the month, Papaji (my grandfather) escorted me to where mummy was at my paternal grandparents' home.

It was a good four months before Daddy recovered sufficiently to look to future plans. Adhering to his doctor's advice, that he should not travel to distant places and should now resume office at Delhi, an application for his immediate transfer from Agartala was made.

Mummy undertook the colossal mission of moving lock stock and barrel from Agartala to the capital, as Daddy was forbidden from undertaking any stressful and difficult tasks. Thus, in April 1970, Sandy and I accompanied Mummy to Agartala to keep her company, while she wound up the house, school, and undertook other formalities; and what a job that must have been! I must say that she managed excellently, and I helped her too by wrapping cups and glasses in newspaper and handing them over to be carefully packed into boxes.

The move of residence was completed by mid-June, and soon, Daddy rejoined work and both Sandy and I were admitted to schools in Delhi. Sandy had secured admission to the Springdale's School, and I had managed to get a place in Loreto Convent.

At the time of my admission, my parents told the principal, Sister Clare, about my vision impairment, plus the few adjustments they might need to make in school for my sake. The kind Irish nun emphatically assured my parents of the school's complete cooperation, and so it proved. I joined Loreto Convent, Delhi, housed in a modern building with locker desks and swinging chairs, armed with a brand new set of books and uniform. At school, the teachers were not only great teachers but also wonderful human beings, as were the angelic Irish nuns.

Although I was among the tall girls in my class, I was allocated a seat in the first row, right in front of the blackboard to facilitate optimum visual access as well as my teacher's attention during class. Even though I could not see the writing on the board, my prominent seat in class provided me with the advantage of concentrating on every word the teachers uttered. My teachers were gifted with the most wonderful common sense and, most naturally it seemed, pronounced aloud every word they wrote on the board. My ears for their part, never failed to catch and engrave upon my brain, the slightest sounds that left their lips.

When it came to writing down answers in our notebooks, I would ask my classmates to read the questions aloud and thereafter, would stick my nose into my notebook and scribble away in whatever handwriting I could muster.

In fact, two very sweet and kindhearted Bengali girls, Anuradha Bhowmik and Dia Banerjee, sat on either side took it upon themselves to help me. They would take turns to copy my homework and notes into my notebooks and if unable to complete the job, they willingly lent me their notebooks to carry home to be copied by Mummy. During the midday break at school, both my dear friends would take me with them and we would sit on the steps outside the classroom or eat our midday snacks under one of the trees in the garden. Gradually, I got to know the rest of the girls in class and school became fun and something I looked forward to.

During the games period, I was included in all the teams and played throwball and basketball, although in formal matches, I voluntarily opted to stand out with the non-players and cheered my class/house team. As far as I was concerned, I felt no different from the other girls. No one girl was like another in the school, and I knew that no one was perfect.

The only mishap relating to school occurred when one fine afternoon I got too involved in chatting with friends on the school bus home and forgot to get off at the appointed stop. This is, however, quite a common occurrence with school kids, and I guess, continues to happen even today.

Why then was I the only one picked upon for dismissal from school? All was going on well, and I, though not topping the class, was not relegated for poor performance. The transfer of dear Sister Clare dramatically altered the course of my life, and the new principal is most certainly one of the people I need to thank for my achievements today. Had she not expelled me from school when she did, I would never have developed the skills I possess.

Well, on the fateful day of my exclusion from formal education, I recall with particular clarity the cane chair at the school's reception area on which I sat brooding. Awaiting my transfer certificate, thinking to myself, 'I will never again come to school again; what have I done to deserve this?' From here on, my memory fades away into deep gloom, to reappear when I am immersed in a paroxysm of heartbreaking sobs that filled the stillness of my home in Sector 3, R.K. Puram. Everything seemed to have come to a full stop: no school, no studies, no play, no friends, and nothing to look forward to.

I went around looking at myself as if from the outside, shrinking at the pitiful words and glances that were floating towards me from all quarters. Sandy was as usual going to school every morning, but I was being left behind with all the doors of life tightly shut in my very face. I would somehow get by in the day, but the nights found me crying myself to sleep. I controlled my weeping tears till I was certain that Sandy had dropped into a deep slumber and only then gave vent to the waves of lonely despair that engulfed my very being. Sometimes, when I wept bitterly into my pillow, Mummy would hear my sobs and run to my bedside to gently console me with her ever encouraging words and love. All the while, I was guiltily aware that my sorrow made my parents, and even little Sandy, very sad, and so I began practising to control my crying as best I could. What I really could not bear was the fact that I brought so much pain to these three people whom I loved more than life. I felt that I had caused them sufficient suffering with my various illnesses and handicap; I must do everything in my power to bring them happiness, and for some reason, that was not immediately possible, I had no right to inflict so much more pain just by weeping away in the way I was. Well, never mind how unhappy and depressed I felt, I decided never to cry in front of anyone ever again.

Then, out of the gloom one day, I caught a glimpse of a ray of hope. It came through a search for a school for the blind, to which I could be admitted to enable me to complete my education. I heard that as no regular school was willing to admit me due to my visual impairment, a school for the blind was the only answer.

A couple of days later, I accompanied my parents to the only school for blind girls in Delhi. Here, I was certain to be taken, so my little dreaming heart came alive once more.

'I will be with other girls and make loads and loads of friends this time,' I thought. 'I will, like other children, go to school and have fun once again.' Then suddenly, I was rudely jerked out of my reverie by the disapproving tone of my mother's voice. She was saying to the principal, 'I will personally bring her to school every day but under no conditions would I like to leave her in the school hostel.'

The rising anticipations crashed straight back into the gloom that had settled upon my world ever since Loreto Convent had shut its doors on me. My thirteen-year-old heart could not fathom the underlying jeopardy in the simple act of allowing me to rejoin school, and I even felt annoyed with Mummy for making such a fuss. 'Other girls were living and studying here in the hostel,' I thought to myself, 'then why was I not being allowed the privilege? At least, I too will once more have a school to go to, and it could very well be exciting to live with friends in school,' I thought.

Nothing of the sort however occurred; instead, we promptly returned home with all plans of sending me to a school for the blind shelved forever. I never had the courage to voice my feelings and thus diminished the ray of hope that had momentarily illuminated the darkness that engulfed my soul.

Time gradually plodded along, and soon, I was offered the proposition of pursuing music as a possible career. I could work towards becoming a music teacher and very easily have a music school of my own. I meekly submitted to the idea, although I never had any great fascination for classical music. Listening to songs over the radio was as far as I had till then ventured in the field of music, and I was more interested in their lyrics than the melody itself. Anyhow, I had to do something and no alternative appeared available.

Mr P.D. Saptarishi, a well-known violinist, was engaged as my music teacher. It was arranged that 'Guruji' would come home twice a week to give me lessons. Guruji advised that it would be good for me to begin studying music by learning vocal music, but I was too self-conscious about my voice, and so I instead chose to learn to play the sitar directly.

I was horrified at the thought of having to sing in front of people! Somewhere deep down within me was the belief that I had a bad voice and there was nothing that could make me open my mouth. I disliked even my speaking voice, so how in heaven could I sing? Instrumental music therefore it had to be.

My music lessons were inaugurated with a solemn prayer to Goddess Saraswati, the goddess of learning, and as I touched the feet of my guruji to obtain his blessings for a bright future ahead, he blessed me with the following words: 'Never ever, as long as you live, my dear child,' he advised, 'should you cease to learn. The day an individual believes and proclaims that s/he knows all, that is the day of her/his nemesis.'

These have ever since been the precious words that from that moment were added to my treasure of golden guiding rules. Somewhere along the way, I took this further by learning from every living and so-called non-living thing in the universe, and did my utmost to harness the knowledge thus garnered into my daily living.

Returning to my music lessons, I earnestly focused upon hard work. I would wake up before dawn each morning, practise as instructed, and do the same for an hour every evening. I then enrolled as a distance-learning student for the Visharad (a six-year diploma course in Indian classical music) at one of India's finest music institutes, the Gandharva Maha Vidyalaya.

The study of music took me into a whole new world of the history of Indian classical music, the ragas and the instruments, and in addition, the life story of the great masters of music, their respective contributions to this enormous field, the success they had achieved, and the dedication and devotion coupled with the effort they had put into bringing to Indian classical Indian music international recognition. This study seemed to ignite within me a passionate desire to follow suit and to become one of the vehicles to carry forward this phenomenal art to new frontiers, as my personal tribute to these supreme masters.

My pursuits began. I listened intently to the life stories of all conceivable masters of music, and then followed my inner voice to replicate as much as I could, the successful trails I learnt from the books. I was well aware that if I desired to achieve success of the magnitude achieved by the masters, I would need to walk in their footsteps, and if possible, work harder than they had.

A part of my music education was to attend classical music and dance performances. The grand auditoriums to which we went for such performances would enchant me with splendid spotlights illuminating the magnificently clad celebrities, almost creating an atmosphere of divinity. I witnessed each of the performances spellbound; nothing escaped my attentive ears and alert mind. The devoted audience, the heartfelt applause, and the pleas for once more, ignited within me the passion to being the recipient of such acclamation. Although I hardly understood or even saw much of the actual music or dance recital, I would be swept away by the surrounding grandeur. Mummy would describe in detail the visual effects on stage in the minutest detail, mentioning with appreciation even the attire and makeup of the artists. The rest was picked up by my other senses through the sounds and vibrations in the atmosphere. My imagination would then stretch its magnificent wings and cruise away on to the stage, and transform me into the performing artist. Oh, and what a feeling that was. I would hear the deafening sound of the applause and then see myself majestically bowing to my admirers, accepting with the elegance of a queen, the flowers and gifts being bestowed upon me.

Long after we came back from these programmes, I lived and relived them in my imagination hundreds of times, and constituted the drive to create this reality for myself, whatever the cost.

By this time, I had made up my mind that I would never ever teach music or have a music school of my own, and would settle for nothing less than performing at par with Shri Ravi Shankar, if not be better. I held in my mind's eye, the picture of me going on stage amidst the cheers of thousands of fans dressed in a pure white silk saree, studded with pearls and diamonds, glittering on the bright illumination of the stage. The motivation this image generated, and the subsequent spellbound silence of my admirers at the sound of the magical melody from my splendid instrument was sufficient to enable me take into my stride, any hardship that may arise in transmuting my dream into reality! With this exhilarating vision in view, I created and followed diligently the programme I had designed for myself, confident of its success.

The journey I embarked upon went as follows. I had learnt that the masters, when they sat down to practise music, lit a big candle and did not stir from their work till this candle had burnt itself out. Well, I wanted to do this too but because I was unable to see, this seemed impractical. I therefore pledged to practise eight hours each day. My guruji advised that riyaaz in the early hours preceding daybreak was most beneficial. I therefore got hold of the alarm clock and set it to 4 a.m. for my first hours of riyaaz.

The album of my memory still echoes the frightening experience of the first morning when the alarm clock shrieked into my slumbering ears. On that bitterly cold morning, the silence following the shrill alarm chilled my very being. I lay dazed under my warm and comfortable quilt, wondering why in heavens name I needed to get out of bed at that unearthly hour. Just as I contemplated the beguiling thought of snuggling deeper into the warm comfort of my bedclothes, my vision and resolve propelled me out of the comfort of the covers! 'You have to get on to that stage,' I told myself, 'so you better move on, my dear Penny, or else your dream will just remain a dream forever.'

Pulling the woollen shawl over my head, I jumped out of bed, slowly feeling my way in the dark I stepped into the drawing room. Not wishing to disturb the sleeping household, I gently shut the door, and settled on to the carpet to embark upon the long and slow journey of diligent struggle to success.

As the musical notes of my instrument filled the small room, a deep sense of purpose and thrill took possession of my world, dissolving into nothingness; my hurting fingers, and the bitter cold. The thought of being the best sitar player in the world provided me with the energy and strength to enjoy every working moment.

●• ●•
●• ••
•• ••

Following this, for years, my riyaaz commenced at 4.30 a.m. and concluded at 5 p.m. Oh yes, I certainly took breaks for meals and to bathe during the day, but then, these too were timed by my big black clock with its bold white numbers and hands.

Following my rapidly improving proficiency in the art, Guruji handed me over to Mr Satish Kumar, a radio artist and a sitar specialist, to take over my tutoring. Life moved smoothly forward, days melting into months, and months into years. I had now completed five years and was in the final year of the course, when my present Guruji was taken ill and could no longer come home to teach. I was thereafter placed under the able guidance of Mr Narendra Nath Ghosh, who was also a well-known radio artist. He said one day, 'This is your final year of the Visharad, my dear, now I am no longer going to spoon-feed you with the notes. You must now play alongside me, listening while I play, and learn to improvise for yourself within the contours of the ragas.'

Sitar in hand, I nervously took my position opposite my guruji, while he fine-tuned his own instrument. The melody soon began to emerge from Guruji's sitar, and his soft voice urged me to follow. For the first time in the five long years of my music education, I was at a complete loss. What in heavens name was I to hear and follow? I could not figure out a single note that Guruji was playing; instead, my head throbbed with indignation at my absolute ineptitude. Guruji, unaware of my plight, thought I was feeling uneasy at this new mode of instruction and kept his composure while he tactfully resorted to playing the basic notations (the first notes of music). Relieved, at being able to recognize the basic notes on the basis of the rigorous practise routine I had been following, I played along. But the moment he began playing complicated compositions, I froze once again!

Guruji put down his instrument and asked me gently, 'What is the matter with you, my dear child? Were you unable to hear and recognize what I was playing?' I shook my head in denial, wondering what punishment I would now be subjected to, having totally failed. 'Do tell me,' he said, his voice almost becoming a whisper, 'how have you been scoring so well in your exams, and, your hand is amazingly perfect on the instrument; how is it possible that a person who can play like that does not recognize the notes?'

I sat feeling completely heart broken, 'Please do give me another chance,' I pleaded, and my lips quivering with the effort of stopping the tears that threatened. 'I honestly have been working very hard, yet I fail to understand, why I can't understand the music.' To this, Guruji thoughtfully replied, 'If you listen to any kind of music regularly, practise earnestly, it automatically happens, my child.' Hope seemed to stir within me once more, and I asked, 'How much should I practise and how long should I listen to music?' 'Oh, you need to practise at least one or two hours in the morning and about the same in the evenings and you can listen to the classical music programmes that come on All India Radio late in the evenings every day.'

By then, my parents had returned from their regular evening stroll while they waited for my coaching to finish. Overhearing our conversation, my mother interjected, 'Preeti practises for at least eight hours daily'. Guruji was totally dumbfounded and, patting my head, affectionately declared, 'So, this explains it. I now understand such perfect performance, and must reveal to you that you do not possess a natural ear for music.' Being a true Guru, he did not wish to delude me about the real situation facing me. He went on further, 'As your teacher, Preeti, it is my duty to guide you with regard to your career in the field of music'. Hesitating, but for a moment only, and speaking softly, 'The way forward for you, as I see it, would be to ultimately choose to take up teaching music as your aim.' I glanced at him sharply, and guessing what was going on in my mind, he went on, 'I know you wish to become a performing artist, but, Preeti, my dear,' he said, 'without an ear for music, it may just not be possible.' Seeing the despair on my face, he quickly added, 'Giving small performances is not for you; please don't take it to heart; you are probably destined to do much greater things in your life.'

I said nothing, as the lump in my throat was too big to swallow; the urge to break down and weep had almost taken over my well-practised calm. I silently pulled the cover over my sitar, rose to my feet, and followed my parents to the car. None of us spoke for a long while, then, Mummy, as always, broke the sad silence with her loving and encouraging words about the present situation. What had happened? I don't remember what she said, because I heard nothing, but I knew she was trying to sooth the excruciating pain that wrenched my insides.

My only dream had been shattered into a million pieces; had been scattered and blown away. There was no way I could ever collect and assemble the pieces because the magic chalice that had contained and nurtured it had lain only in my imagination. The popular myth, which must have captivated many a blind person before me, and will do so long into the future, had beguiled me too: 'When God takes away a person's eyesight, he makes an unfailing gift of an ear for music.' Where was mine? I demanded from God, feeling utterly suffocated and frozen. Also, if He had decided not to gift me an ear for music, why did He plant such a dream in my heart!

That night, I lay awake in bed, speculating miserably over all that had passed over these past five years, and all I could conjure was one big jumble. Why had my dreams once again crashed? This time, I had done more than my best to make realize them; what had I done to deserve so much failure? Why me?

Nothing except music had ever been a part of my life and now that there was no music to keep me occupied, a peculiar sense of emptiness took hold. There was only pain and despair to be had this way. How much should I cry and mourn? Before long, I realized I was getting nowhere in this way and began to think, 'Either I cry and cry for the rest of my days over split milk, or begin to look for something positive'. I silently scolded myself, 'My crying will only break Mummy's and Daddy's hearts, and so it may be better instead to find ways of finding happiness. As it is, I seem to be a constant source of worry and concern to them; and it is about time I at least avoid creating a situation of greater pain and grief for them. If I think hard enough, I will manage to find something that will provide an alternative to weeping.'

So it was that night and many other nights from then onwards, I persisted in my search for positive things, in order to divert my aching mind from the adversity, and it was not long before I began to uncover various fascinating occurrences whose significance had been dulled by the flame of my dedication to music. My thoughts drifted about and slowly rested on the other major but unnoticed activities and changes that had simultaneously accompanied me through my teens.

I soon began feeling good about the moments when I would, in between learning music, lend my mother a hand in the house, sometimes dusting, sometimes learning the art of cooking, and watering the small back garden, and at others ironing. I had also mastered the art of making of our beds, setting and keeping our room tidy, especially on days when the housemaid was on leave.

From the day I made this resolve, the gloom began lifting, and my attention began to fall upon some wonderful things to which I had attached very little importance when I was single mindedly occupied by my mission in music. Now that this had undergone a change, I automatically focused on events and experiences that on their own were quite delightful and significant.

As I traced my footsteps down the memory lane of the five long years immersed in music, I must certainly have been conscious of my other passion, which was frozen in the pain and indignation that arose in the face of such a colossal failure. True, many suggestions and pieces of advice were being offered, but my mind was made up. I would do riyaaz just sufficiently to get through my examination and obtain a diploma, but nothing would now or ever in the future persuade me to teach music. In my heart, it was amply clear to me that I would never be able to become a teacher, given my lack of sight. If I myself was unable to decipher notes, how would I be able to teach anyone else?

I therefore continued to live in the way I felt comfortable with, and searched for my true passion and inspiration. What people said did upset me very much, but I seemed stuck with the notions inside my head.

My parents tried to persuade me to resume my schooling and offered to find me a distant learning option, but that too did not appeal to me. 'What will I do with a few new certificates and a few degrees?' I remonstrated haughtily. I was not interested in studying subjects that would be of no practical use to me, 'and, anyway, I don't wish to take up a job, and would prefer to get married and raise a family instead,' I argued. 'And, I love to learn and read,' I grumbled, 'knowledge is all that is essential, and that I am gathering all the time.'

It was much later in life that I was able to gauge the torment to which I was subjecting my dear parents and, as you read on, you will realize the challenges I was creating for myself. Now, I would like you to accompany me through my memories of the various events that took place alongside the time when I was enwrapped in, and enraptured by music.

During these years, medical technology had advanced sufficiently for magnifying glasses of '50^X', to be fitted into a spectacle frame. This was a windfall for me, because with them, I could read some printed material in a controlled environment. Of course, it was difficult to read even under these circumstances because the spectacles would only magnify text from a distance of approximately three inches; when the light was adjusted on the text from an angle behind my head.

Therefore, in order to read, one held the material in both hands in close proximity to the nose, while both elbows precariously swung in mid-air to achieve the required position. This of course necessitated a high degree of endurance from all the muscles involved in the exercise: arms and neck. In addition, there was the jugglery of keeping closed the fluttering eyelid that was not to be used in the exercise. Only when all this was successfully achieved would the reading get underway utilizing the smarting, watering open eye. Even though, one was obliged to choose books that were printed in dark black ink with a large clear font, on pure white paper; reading independently became possible. Soon, reading became my first love, opening up to me an entirely new world. In this new world, I experienced the thrill of independently exploring new fields of knowledge, which had till then only been possible through the radio and movie sound tracks.

Seeing my interest in reading, and to spice up my life somewhat, Mummy gave me a romance by Denise Robbins titled *The Leopard in the Snow*. I thoroughly enjoyed my very first love story. Ashley, the name of the 'tall, dark and handsome' hero of this story even now evokes happy memories, and as a consequence, a new dream was born.

Suddenly, I became pleasantly conscious of my own youthful womanhood and began paying attention to my appearance: 'What was it that would attract someone like Ashley into my life?' I wondered. Although I was tall at 5 feet 7 inches, with a fair complexion and long, lightly wavy dark brown hair, my frame seemed to slouch with a layer of unsightly fat. Once I had cognized these negative attributes, I was perturbed and soon slipped into a painful depression when the words 'Ashley couldn't take his eyes off her tall slender figure,' resonated in my mind. This realization, however, made it self-evident to me that if I wished any Ashley to surrender his heart to me, I had to acquire that 'slender figure'! To make matters worse, Mummy too advocated the undoubted charm of 'a slim, trim figure'. She would always say, 'You know Penny, you would have all the attributes of the most attractive young girl in town, if only you could knock off the extra kilos.'

Then, she would continue encouragingly, 'You are so pretty you know, and also such an intelligent and bright person, that if we could trim off the excess weight, no one would bother about your vision impairment! Everyone has negative aspects, and yours is your eyesight,' she always said with a confident smile, 'and, when all the rest of your positive qualities sparkle, the one defect you have to live with will be become insignificant. Hardly anyone focuses on the defects of the sun or the moon,' she would say, 'people simply enjoy the unlimited benefits they offer! So, my darling,' she would coax, 'look for ways of developing and perfecting all your positive traits, and always be of value to others, and the universe will be truly yours! Endeavour to give to others, rather than opportunities for seeking favours!' These words of profound wisdom made a permanent impression upon my character and from then on, I literally lived by its every word.

With no school to go to and no inclination to labour over music practice, time was at my disposal to be spent as I wished. Yes, reading did occupy a good deal of my time, but I still had a lot to spare.

In this relaxed spare time, I slept a lot, chatted with my best friend over the phone, and constantly indulged myself with food. In order to prevent me from eating my way to destruction, and keep myself occupied gainfully, Mummy very tactfully began drawing me into her household chores. She would get me to help her with things like cooking, cleaning, washing up, and dusting (which I most disliked). Besides, I was entrusted with the responsibility of hand-knitting borders for the sweaters and pullovers Mummy knitted on her knitting machine for her clients. She had taken up this home-based business to help my father with some extra income for the family. At this time too, I was cajoled to join my parents on their regular long early morning walks.

Sometimes, when I found myself at a loose end, as most teenage girls do, I would sneak away to the dressing table, to pose and model innovative hairstyles with my long hair, apply cosmetics, adorn myself with trinkets, and rehearse a private fashion show. I spent countless hours enjoying the challenge of draping my mother's saris around me: the five and a half-six meter of material that constitutes the Indian national dress for women. It was that I did take some time out for that when I did, because today most of my friends can't drape it as well as I do.

Other than these moments of small pleasures, life continued uneventfully, barring visits to the hospital and an occasional trip to the movies with my mom. You will agree that getting out of bed early is difficult, especially on cold foggy, wintery mornings. But the unrelenting pressure from my parents had the effect of getting me to reluctantly get out of the cozy comfort of bed to become the third member of their morning walk party.

As soon as my booted feet stepped outdoors, the effort usually proved worthwhile. The fresh morning air and chirping birds would promptly infuse me with unbounded energy and enthusiasm. Through the IIT campus or the sprawling wilderness of the then developing JNU grounds, we walked, trying to outrace the swarms of flies that desperately struggled to obtain a free ride on our shoulders. Both these campuses were across the road from our Sector 3, R.K. Puram home and, hosts of health-conscious people came regularly for a walk, yoga, or to jog. Among these were a large number of fitness-enthusiastic students from the two renowned universities too, evoking in me a longing to be a student myself. An agonizing desire it was, because for me, the prospect of a university education was entirely out of the question! To conceal my sorrow and the shame of being incomplete, together with a desire to protect my loving parents from suffering utter helplessness and pain at my plight, I would desperately suppress my tears, plant a bright smile on my face, and would concentrate on the fun stories and other interesting things I would get to hear. My parents too put into words, all they observed, which almost made me forget that I could not see what was happening around us. The conversation went on something like this: 'The sun is looking like a huge orange red ball' or 'it is so foggy today that one can hardly see the people walking on the other side of the road.' Alternatively, 'You see this couple walk their feet off, and then they engage in all these complicated yoga asanas, and yet they always look a few kilos fatter every time we see them.' 'The, bird you hear there has everything brown, but its feet are such a pretty yellow. You know, they say, once upon a time this little brown birdie was invited to a wedding and was very sad because she looked so plain. She therefore went to the peacock and begged him to exchange his feet with her just for the wedding, so that she would have at least something to show off there. The trusting peacock complied, the feet were exchanged, and as you may have guessed, the little brown bird never again returned the lovely yellow feet. That's why the peacock is such a beautiful bird with such ugly feet and this plain Jane little birdie has the pretty yellow ones for keeps.'

Stories and comments such as these, along with conscious information sharing discussions during this early morning walk played a vital role in shaping most of my values and beliefs. On school holidays, our morning walks would be converted into picnic/adventure expeditions, as Sandy would come along. I can't move on without giving you a peek into some of the interesting and daring things Sandy and I got into doing out of our shared love of fun and adventure.

Once on a fiercely cold and misty early January morning, sharp at 6 a.m., our family of four stepped onto the street for our morning walk. Dawn was still a long way off, the roads virtually deserted barring some fellow morning walkers or milk-fetchers passing by. Generally enthused and full of life, we kids trotted alongside our parents, playfully blowing into the icy cold, and then chasing the tiny clouds, our warm breath created beneath the pale yellow light of the street lamps. This would normally entice Daddy into explaining the scientific phenomena, followed by his favourite account of his warm breath freezing on his beard in the icy winter air in the USA, how his lips were sealed by his frozen beard, and how he had to return to the hotel and wash his face with hot water to melt away his frozen beard before he was able to speak again.

I remember being intrigued with this story and made various fruitless attempts to form ice on my own face too.

Once we entered the traffic-free IIT campus, Sandy and I were free to walk without supervision and usually exercised our freedom by running up ahead or trailing behind the little walking party. We were both great friends, though Sandy was almost a foot and a half shorter than my tall, stout self, and yet he kept me in splits whenever we were on our own together. He had a fantastic talent of bringing alive, in my head, stories and occurrences of the present or past in an extremely dramatic manner. Thus, laughing and talking, we made up our own private walking party separated from our parents. On one such morning walk, the early morning mist gave way to a heavy fog as the sun rose, enveloping everything within a thick shroud. Although we were just a few steps behind our parents, they were fast becoming invisible in the quickly gathering fog. As soon as visibility dropped to zero and the existence of other humans could only be deciphered by the sounds they made, Sandy said he was not able to see anything except his own hand in front and me beside him. We heard our parents call to us to come up alongside them, so that we could keep close together in the heavy fog. Sandy and I however had other plans: we had already resolved to let them walk ahead and gradually get sort of lost. This would be fun, just like being lost in the desert or in a wilderness of snow. The plan was so exciting that we lost no time in reassuring Mummy and Daddy that we were able to follow them quite well and they need not worry that we would get left behind. Then, rapidly slowing down, and, also taking a few steps backwards, we actually were, in no time at all, completely beyond their earshot. For a few minutes, it was quite thrilling to be on our own in a city like Delhi, with Mummy and Daddy out of earshot actually felt like a true adventure! A short while later, however, the 'true adventure' became a 'really frightening experience'; the total loss of visibility completely baffled us, and we found ourselves truly lost. The next half hour was spent wondering what we should do if we never ever got home, but fortunately it never got that far. This experience did not for a moment discourage our adventure-seeking passion, and a few months later, in the Dharampur hills, Sandy and I spent a good part of four hours jumping from rock to rock and foothold to foothold on the steep hillside. On one particular day, we decided to go for our after breakfast walk to Dagro Pull, traversing the valley rather than following the proper Sabathu road which led to it. On this occasion of course, we did not get lost as it was a bright and sunny day, but, we certainly returned home more than a touch dazed, famished, and thirsty, with hurting hands and feet, to be greeted by a houseful of worried grown-ups.

'Where have you two been?' asked my mother and grandmother in unison. 'We just as usual went walking to Dagro,' Sandy clarified. 'But it does not take four hours to go and come back from Dagro,' scolded my grandmother, 'it is already past 2 o' clock… where have you two been?'

'Oh, yes, it took us a little long because we went to Dagro by the "adventure trail" because we wanted to be in real touch with the hillside, just like the people did in the olden days,' I explained, trying to make these oldies see our point of view. 'And where is the "adventure trail" may I know?' asked my mother in bewilderment. 'We made one up for ourselves,' Sandy hurried to clarify, 'by jumping off the roadside on to the hillside and climbing down in the direction of Dagro. Because then it turned out to be a very long route and we thought you would all be worried, we decided to turn back before even reaching there.' 'And how did you both get back in one piece,' the astounded ladies wanted to know in utter amazement. 'Oh, no problem, I kept jumping ahead off the hillsides and Penny jumped behind me where she heard me fall, and if she slipped, I simply caught her fast,' answered the innocent boy. 'And how did that help with you half her size?' Then turning on me, she asked, 'How did you just allow yourself to be led into such dangerous pranks by this little rascal?' Well, that is where the matter ended, as we both promised, without actually meaning it, not to repeat it and also apologized profusely for our so-called foolish adventure trip. The next time we repeated something like that, we learnt to cover up our tracks better.

Round about the same time, I discovered the portable typewriter which Daddy had brought from the US, lying around the house. I was as usual attracted to the gadget and wondered if it would be possible for me to learn to use it. A little deliberation and investigation into this matter confirmed that I could learn to touch type; and therefore located and joined an old-style typing institute near our home. I had now found a way of communicating independently in a legible script, just as others did. Once I had mastered the skill, I had bridged that gap and was at par with the sighted world in this sphere too. I could of course have fulfilled my desire to write independently, using the Braille script, but that would never have served the purpose of establishing a link with the world where I was actually to survive. How could my family and friends read a letter written in Braille? And how were they to reply to me in the intricate dotted script? I probably would have to find blind relatives and friends and then later go to the land of the blind to exercise my social skills and obligations. Unfortunately, no matter what is said and believed about teaching and training persons with disabilities in special ways, we eventually have to coexist in this one world with all its inhabitants. At least one thing was firmly established in my mind that I always wanted to learn and do things that were learnt and done by the people with whom I lived. Yes, I do confess, the teaching methodology for many tasks was most of the time adapted to my specific requirement. However that may be, I very earnestly set about practising the art of typing with all ten fingers; nothing would stop me from running in tandem with those surrounding me.

I never allowed the handicap of not being able to read and type simultaneously become a constraint in mastering typing skills. Rather, I accepted it as a challenge, and formulated an innovative strategy to surmount this central problem by typing self-constructed sentences for the purpose of practice. I wrote about the day, the weather, the city, the family, and anything else I could imagine effortlessly and swiftly;

and of course, there would be letters that would not only give me the pleasure of communicating my side of the stories and news, but elicit exciting responses as well. Interestingly, replies to my letters with positive feedback, from my grandfathers were indicators of the quality of my writing. My paternal grandfather very earnestly marked out in red ink all the words I had not spelt correctly, and would thereafter return my letters with the corrections to me accompanied by his reply.

Soon, the sound of the keys clicking on the paper fitted on the roller was like music to my ears, and the ever-increasing speed of the flight of my fingers on the keyboard was quite wonderful. This gave me an enormous sense of freedom and accomplishment once I had mastered the contraption. Now, I could write just like everyone else, in complete contrast to the terrible sense of defeat and helplessness I was consumed with in relation to so many other things.

As you proceed with this narrative, you will discover the enormous advantage my typing proficiency eventually proved to be. You may also recall that this was about the time when I had started using my magnifying spectacles; and by this time, I had acquired considerable proficiency in reading with the aid of this incredible device. The enchanting capacity of being able to read and write legible text independently, gave an entirely new dimension and control over my life, and in addition, completely altered my outlook and my position in society, and made me feel in the 'seventh heaven'.

Very rapidly, my self-confidence and self-esteem soared, and banished to obscure recesses of the past, as was the grief and trauma of being ejected from school and the pain and disappointment of my crushed desire to achieve recognition in the field of music.

With every passing moment bringing new experiences, the tiny river of my life, grew deeper and wider. Consequently, precipitous waterfalls, jagged cliffs, and unexpected shocks replaced the little waves, small rocks, and mild rapids that had thus far distressed me. Nonetheless, the gratification of stepping into adulthood, too, brought a beguiling zeal that impelled me to welcome with open arms every change and opportunity.

We had moved out of the Sector 3 flat into a beautiful apartment in Sector 13 in the same colony. This change of residence made available to both Sandy and me the luxury of independent rooms. There was now greater privacy, and more space to allow both of us an independent expression of our individual identity and enhanced freedom, and in addition all the other benefits that accompany a brand new neighbourhood.

Soon after we had settled into our new home, Aunty Topsy (the aunt we had visited in the Silchar tea gardens) came to stay with us for the birth of her baby. She shared my room and enjoyed the daily tantrums that ensued as a consequence of the unsatisfactory fluctuations of the needle of my weighing machine, as I was desperately struggling to lose the unsightly kilos. I weighed myself every morning, and my mood for the day was solely dependent on the little machine's verdict. Aunty Topsy to this day bursts into peals of laughter recalling my tantrums even on days when the needle showed a gain of a few grams!

A month later, aunty was blessed with a bonny baby girl, who was named Komal. Not too long after her arrival, my maternal grandfather, Papa, invited me to accompany him to Calcutta for a short holiday. I was of course overjoyed with the prospect of visiting my favourite aunt, as the frequency of such pleasant times had decreased considerably since we permanently moved out of Agartala. When Aunty Frauke got to hear of our plans, she invited me to stay with them for at least a year. 'Now that you don't have your music lessons to go to,' she said, 'I would love to have you stay with me for at least a year.' I naturally jumped at the invitation, and my parents too agreed to this as I guess, their sole motivation was to see me happy.

So off I went along with Papaji, on one of my life's most significant moves, which gave upon my 'ever ready to soak up' persona, everlasting impressions and experiences. My exceptional Calcutta holiday began with the regular shopping trips, visits to the zoo and restaurants, and a few dinner parties in my grandfather's honour. Although we all loved Papaji dearly, we were excited to be free of his stern, formal demeanor, when he returned to Chandigarh after his 10-day vacation. I had to continue to face the other short-tempered person of the family (my Uncle Surjeet), but there were Aunty Frauke and six-year old Sabine to compensate for that.

It was to be my seventeenth birthday and as a birthday present, my aunt got me a pair of jeans, some tops, and my first ever haircut. I always wanted my hair to resemble those of the girl in a picture from a magazine (I had kept the cutting stashed away and constantly peered at it). Then, as all my dreams had learnt to come true, we went to the hairdressers and I came away an hour later feeling like a princess. Nothing, absolutely nothing, had the power to cast the slightest shadow over the sense of loveliness that overcame me and adoration of my newfound image with the hairdo of my dreams. The fact that I was overweight and had a major disability ceased to mar this in the least. Incidentally, 'Pretty Preeti' was the title of Mr Khushwant Singh's write-up about me in his column.

Rapidly and effortlessly, the routine of my foster home grew on me. Each morning, I would rise to share my morning tea with Aunty Frauke, as she had her breakfast before she left for work at half past seven in the morning. Shortly thereafter, Uncle Surjeet would leave for his office and Sabine too left for school. I would be left to amuse myself till about midday, when Sabine returned, and it would not be very long before Aunty Frauke also joined us. Thereafter, we would customarily spend the rest of the afternoon either at the Calcutta Swimming Club, go shopping, or visit friends.

Up to this time, I had never had the opportunity of learning to swim and indeed had a major phobia about water. Even under the shower in the bathroom, I kept my face away from the fine spray in the apprehension that I might drown. Now, however, as I was ever so often at the swimming club, watching everyone enjoy the sport, it seemed a good idea to learn to swim. Aunty Frauke of course promised I would be alright with her beside me; and additionally tempted me with the assertion that it was the best form of exercise and also so much fun. I agreed to learn to swim, and counseled my fluttering heart: 'This is a wonderful opportunity to trim off some of the horrid fat off my back, and I might even become a champion swimmer and make a mark in the swimming world.'

Mind made up, I was fitted with a beautiful blue and red swimsuit and timidly began taking swimming lessons from my aunt. My fear of drowning wasn't however, taking me very far. To make matters worse, I would often find myself under water, as my cousin and her little friends found it very amusing to swim around me like mermaids, while I struggled to hang on to a rubber ball to keep myself afloat.

Observing my fruitless efforts at the swimming pool, one of my aunt's German colleagues, volunteered to take on the challenge of coaching me. Oh boy, what a coach he proved to be; he efficiently freed me from my little mermaids and with Aunty Frauke cheering by our side, I was on my way. Under Mr Kerna's expert guidance, I was afloat without support within two days and swam my first length non-stop on the ninth day. I must confess, I was scared stiff each time we swam into the deep end, but Aunty Frauke and Mr Kerna swam beside me and kept me going. Fascinatingly, it was this dear Mr Kerna who must also be given the credit for my present supreme confidence on the dance floor. This happened shortly after our brief swimming acquaintance, at a fancy dress dinner party. I felt myself being firmly, yet purposefully, drawn off my nervous perch on a high bar stool. Before I could make anything of the sudden alteration in my state, I was swirling away in time with the melodious waltz, firmly ensconced in the strong and capable strong arms of this tall German. Then, as the music changed to a German folk tune, I suddenly found myself being danced like a rubber doll, into the merrily bobbing crowd of frisking men and women. Holding hands sometimes, grabbing shoulders at others, frolicking in and out of strange human formations, getting swung from elbow to arm and, amazingly, all of me remained in one piece, and through some divine miracle, I landed back into the firm arms of my original partner.

To the onlookers and to those who were dancing along, it all must have seemed very natural, as if I had twirled around every day of my life, swaying expertly to the beats on the dance floor, with my feet hardly ever making contact with the ground. For my part, I was completely swept off; for a moment I was dizzy with panic, and the next, I discovered enormous pleasure could be derived on the dance floor, provided one was being escorted there and partnered by a dancer as skilled, sophisticated, and polished as Mr Kerna.

The shy and uncertain young girl that I was, I am quite certain that I would never have dared to venture anywhere near such activities for the fear of being ridiculed or pitied. Now, given the slightest retest and opportunity, I am the first one on the dance floor and inside a swimming pool, and have to be physically dragged away from either. Swimming and dancing is now, for me, like a potent drug and 'what will people think or say?' never bothers me. I have even won a few prizes on the dance floor.

Oh, before you begin to have ideas, let me tell you; my feelings for dear Mr Kerna were absolutely platonic. Up to now, his intentions have been a mystery to me and, anyhow, at that time, I was too flabbergasted and naive to even as much experience any other feelings barring admiration and gratitude towards the good soul. I don't remember ever having a conversation of any kind with dear Mr Kerna;

all that I do remember are the one-word instructions in the water and the polite 'Thank you' after the memorable dance, as he deposited me safely into an exquisitely soft and comfortable sofa. Never after that evening have I had the opportunity to thank him for the enormous part he played in the formation of my personality. I would now therefore like to pay him a heartfelt tribute for his contribution to my development via my book.

As always, every trip to Calcutta brought with it a host of novel experiences, fresh opportunities, and new acquaintances. I was introduced to Mekhola, stepdaughter of my aunt's colleague Renata. Mekhola had just about then completed her schooling in Dehradun, and was waiting for college to open. Both of us took to each other right from the outset and soon, we were spending a lot of time together. Through Mekhola, I met a host of other young people, and, if you please, was also invited to my first date.

This was, I must confess, a very pleasant shock. I had heard of dating, but had never dared to even dream of being dated myself, and that too by a medical student. As you may recall, I had been very closely associated with doctors, from a patient's standpoint, and was much enamored by the medical profession and all those associated with it. It was therefore extremely flattering to have a 'doctor in the making', find me attractive enough, and that too, in the face of all my flab, plus a disability, to actually ask me out. I felt no less elated on that day than Cinderella must have felt when the Prince actually came looking for her and whisked her off to be his bride.

Well, I secured permission from both my guardians to go out with Govind, without a hitch, and again I was most pleasantly overwhelmed. In fact, Uncle Surjeet drove me to Park Hotel on Park Street himself, and there, Govind met me at the appointed place.

Getting out of the car, I walked alongside my newly acquired boyfriend, assuming an apparent confidence which effectively concealed the acute sense of nervousness that bubbled within. We entered the dimly lit, sparsely populated coffee shop, housed in the well-known 5 star hotel in the heart of Calcutta.

Govind led me to a table for four, and helped me on to the sofa adjoining the wall, sliding on to the same sofa next to me. Tiny bells of alarm tinkled inside my head as he continued to slide himself on that damned sofa, till he was half lying on it, with his head (thankfully) resting on the low back of the seat, about two feet away from mine! Sighing with relief, it was time to place our order, and what a disappointment that proved: only a 'hot chocolate' for me and a coffee for him. I had at least looked forward to some good food at such a snazzy hotel. Little did I realize then that dating Govind meant only one cup of hot chocolate or coffee.

Well, while we awaited refreshments, I took a closer look at my silent companion lying beside me, wondering what a curious looking couple we made, for by then, my eyes had adjusted to the comfortable dim lighting of the room, and I saw for the first time (whatever I could see), my south Indian companion. He was as thin as a matchstick, as dark as the night, and a piteous contrast to well fed, tall, and majestic young woman seated beside him. He hardly uttered more than a few words throughout the hour and a half that we were there; it was I who kept a conversation of sorts going between of us. And soon, I began to wonder, why I was out with this guy anyway, I did not think that I could have been in love with this man, but probably the motivating factor was that he was a medical student, and had asked me out for a date.

Well, nothing else of note happened during this outing, not even a holding of hands. Mind you, I was sort of glad in a way; I would have to counsel myself a great deal to be able to come to terms with the idea of taking this relationship anywhere at all. On this note, we bade each other a dull goodbye at the gate of my aunt's home. Oh no, this was not the final end. I even dared to get off the Rajdhani train when it stopped at the Dhanbad station for a few minutes, to stand on the platform and talk with this supposed boyfriend, and, wait, there is more to it. We wrote to each other over the next few months and then, one fine day, on his way home to his village, he stopped over at Delhi to be able to see me. Once more, he asked me out, and this time to a 'coffee shop' in Ashoka Hotel in Delhi. The play repeated itself; though this time thankfully, there was no sofa to slide on; so we sat opposite each other and ordered hot chocolate and coffee. He hardly said a word, I jabbered and jabbered, and was dropped back home.

I had had enough of this charade of ridiculous dating with the pitiful medical student; I eventually stopped replying to his silly letters and so came to a close my first 'love affair'. It left me with greater confidence and self-esteem than I had originally had, and as with every new thing, a broader perspective.

Well, back in Calcutta, apart from my own circle of friends, there was an abundance of social interaction. As my uncle was serving as Export General Manager in GEC, this position entailed a host of entertaining. Then there were my aunt's circle of friends, and of course her official contacts with whom to socialize. Although my little cousin was normally left out of the evening parties, I was usually invited to most of those to which my guardians were invited.

Initially, I was nervous and shy at these posh functions, but in due course, as I got to know people, I quite looked forward to them. Besides, in any case, there was usually in addition, good food and music to be enjoyed at these get-togethers. I got to meet loads of interesting people from all over the world, possessing a variety of remarkable characteristics from diverse cultures and backgrounds in such a short span of time in a single city. This extraordinary exposure was a great learning experience for me.

Before I move on to other events and places in this narrative, I would like you to accompany me to one of the most eventful formal dinner parties I attended at the Calcutta Rowing Club (a very posh and happening club at the time). We were invited by a certain Mr and Mrs Green.

Dressed in a plain orange sari, feeling very poised and elegant, I walked into the beautiful clubhouse with my arm linked through my aunt's. We were greeted in the lounge by a very handsome yet stiff upper-lipped English couple who led us to a cozy corner specially booked for the evening. Drinks were ordered, and I shyly asked for a shandy, which I thought would make me appear grown up. The conversation was so low-toned that I could barely hear most of it, and given the fact that I could not read the body language of those sitting there; things got a little uphill for me. Somehow, I managed to look with it (I thought). Hoping desperately that some of the other guests to join the five-some to enable me to conveniently melt into the crowd, I soon realized that this was only wishful thinking. There were only us, and no one else had been invited. I had not until then ever experienced such embarrassment, so the evening dragged on with soft music playing, and the cool Calcutta winter breeze making the atmosphere even more electric. With my face flushing and my hands trembling, dinnertime somehow arrived. Sighing with relief, I thought that now at least the attention of the group would focus on the food, and I could then relax.

The next shock came with the discovery that we were to be seated at a formal dinner table in an almost deserted dining room. 'Oh Lord, how would I manage to handle all the cutlery and crockery,' I groaned to myself, my head spinning with nervousness. I did not want to make a spectacle of myself by not handling the cutlery in the proper way because that would only make everyone pity me. I was no poor little thing and I would not allow any situation to evoke that feeling in anyone. I therefore gathered my senses together with a tremendous effort and managed to sit at the table looking quite composed.

So far, so good. I once again comforted myself that it was all right and everything was going OK until dinner was served. The soup disposed itself into me with alacrity, but the huge stake, jacket potatoes, and peas, triggered off the ordeal. What was I to do now? It would be bad manners to use my fingers, but how on earth could I even begin to get going. I felt all eyes fix upon me, the atmosphere around me seemed to stiffen, and I felt I was being ridiculed by everyone. There seemed no choice but to hastily reach for the cutlery and get cracking. I still remember eating a few bits of the potatoes with the skin still on, and managing clumsily to chop a few bits off the steak. Of course I had to do away with the peas, because there was no point of making a total fool of myself by attempting to get my knife and fork into the tiny green balls that rolled around the plate. I was starving and there was such a lavish spread on my plate, but just imagine my plight. Mrs Green, our hostess, asked if I were not well, or if I did not like the food. I risked a shaky smile and said I was not very hungry and a very small eater (all lies, of course). After what seemed like ages, we rose from the table and said our thank yous and good-byes; thank God the party was behind us.

This awkward experience induced me to master the art of using the cutlery at the dining table. Practice I did, and though I manage to kind of pull through with the knife and fork business on my plate, I have found a simpler way around this difficulty. I simply have stopped pretending to be the Goddess of perfection, and instead seek assistance and don't have to return famished from anywhere again. Over the years, I have found that, asking for help can very easily save you a lot of embarrassment, and can indeed become a shorter and smoother route to inclusion in society.

The hectic hustle and bustle of life with my dear relatives and friends scarcely left me time or occasion to feel any symptom of homesickness. Then suddenly, out of the blue, one evening, the news of Uncle Surjeet being hospitalized jolted me out of my happy existence. He was to undergo an emergency surgery of the spleen and gall bladder, and before he was able to return home, Aunty Frauke landed up in hospital too with a back injury, leaving Sabine and me to fend for the house and ourselves. Thank heavens we had Sabine's maid Teresa and the cook to look after us. Aunty Frauke was hospitalized for a good six weeks, and even after she returned home, she was bedridden most of the time. Despite all efforts, her condition did not improve and she decided to return to Germany for better and more advanced medical treatment. The end of August 1976 saw my aunt and cousin leave for Germany and on 7 September, a few days after that, I too returned home to Delhi.

I travelled without an escort in the Rajdhani for the first time ever. Once on the train, I perched my suitcase on the upper berth along with my sitar and clutched on to my handbag to ensure the safety of my belongings. You see, I had gained ample confidence during the past few months, which made me feel a sense of excitement and responsibility rather than apprehension through the 17-hour journey! Just as the train began rolling away from the platform and picking up speed, my heartbeat did exactly the same. I was returning home to my beloved parents and brother after so long and that too with a complete makeover, with a brand new appearance and so much to relate. Please don't forget either that I was also going to meet my 'boyfriend' at the Dhanbad station.

The hours in the train sped rapidly by, and I found myself in the arms of my eagerly waiting family at New Delhi railway station. They all appeared different, especially Sandy! He was almost as tall as me and had grown up as well. I was pleasantly surprised and delighted at the change these seven months had wrought. It was as if life had turned a new leaf, and I could scarcely relate to the time before I had left for

Calcutta. Past years seemed to be a lifetime away, and today, I was an utterly changed individual.

Bubbling with enthusiasm, I talked non-stop, eager to share all my experiences with my equally excited listeners. I had come back home, more polished, more confident and self-assured, and courtesy the excellent food I had been gorging, heavier by at least five kilos.

At home, there were many pleasant surprises awaiting me. One such revelation was that Mummy had found part-time employment with a market research company. She was no longer confined to home all of the time as her work, though part-time, took her away for long hours on the days she worked. This new setup was hard on me, because, home for me simply meant Mummy, and it was rather strange and unpleasant to have her going out regularly. Therefore, in order, to simply avoid the loneliness, some days I would tag along with her on her door-to-door survey trips. The hardship of accompanying my mother got the better of my then shallow endurance, and I began having second thoughts about accompanying her. The discomfort of commuting in crowded buses and walking from office to office along potholed streets in the extreme Delhi weather was reason enough to soon persuade me to remain in the comfort of home. However, following the fun-filled busy time I had got accustomed to in Calcutta, I was consumed by sheer boredom and restlessness. The long absence from home had put me out of circulation, and I yearned to occupy myself with writing letters and daydreaming.

Gradually, I became acquainted with young people around our building that I met on my frequent visits to the letter-box room downstairs, and got invited to join in the dance parties and other fun events happening around the block. I in fact experimented with Transcendental Meditation too, and most unsuccessfully practised it for a couple of weeks.

At around the same time, my dearest childhood friend from Agartala, Madhumita, moved into the neighbourhood. She was pursuing her graduation from the Delhi University, and through her, I too caught glimpses and flavours of college life. Madhu would often take me along to the college festivals and other social events and proudly present me to her college mates rather than feel ashamed of bringing along a blind girl as her friend. I say this because in general, normal people are known to be embarrassed to proclaim any association whatsoever with persons with disabilities; but this was never the case here. We share a priceless bond, which has, to this day cemented our friendship, through the vicissitudes of life, and whether near or far away, our friendship supersedes the bounds of time and space.

Concluding my very first love affair had left me with a burning urge for a good life partner. Husband hunting had begun in the family for my generation, as a number of my cousins had reached 'marriageable age'. A few of them had already tied the knot and the elders were on the job of finding suitable matches for the others. Although I myself was fast approaching my eighteenth birthday, there was no sign of any 'husband hunting' for me. This was a bit strange, as it was a trend to marry off the daughters of the family as soon as possible; I wondered why was my turn not coming?

Well, turn or no turn, my current ambition in life was to marry and settle down. Therefore, rather than waiting around for someone to find me a husband, I promptly decided to look for one myself. Besides, I alone could choose correctly as I had in my mind's eye the exact picture of the life partner I sought. I was in fact quite satisfied with the turn of events, as this would keep me safe from marrying the wrong person through sheer politeness and a sense of obedience.

Every young unmarried man/boy I met was subjected to careful observation to see if he measured up to my predetermined criterion. Out of the factors that was to be scrupulously avoided was that the prospective groom should not be a Sikh with long hair and a beard, and of course, medical professionals were to receive top billing.

I looked everywhere; in the neighbourhood, among friends, relations, and acquaintances, for the man who was to be given my hand. Although there were some attractive young men I really fancied, to my utter disappointment, nothing seemed to click. Time went by, with a few one-sided crushes and a great deal of daydreaming and hoping against hope for a miracle to occur. That continued until, one day, I discovered the 'Pen Pal' column in *Sun* magazine.

As luck would have it, there was the name of a 'Medico' seeking a friend. Oh yes, of course, I lost no time in pounding out a 'hello' letter to Narandra. I wrote all about myself, including my disability, and within three days, back came an affectionate reply from Madras. Overjoyed at such a quick positive response, I too replied by return post. Before I realized it, letters were flying between Delhi and Madras at breakneck speed. I made 'letter-box room' trips every few hours, and sometimes, had the pleasure of receiving more than a letter a day.

I have no recollection about when or how this 'pen pal' friendship transmuted into a raving 'letter love affair'. Then, as is invariably the case, letters were not sufficient; we longed to meet 'in person' as soon as possible. How was this meeting to come about with over a thousand miles between us? He was besides, too busy to travel, weighted down as he was with the pressure of the final term of medical college; and there seemed no prospect of my travelling alone simply to meet him. But you know, when there is a will, there always comes a way.

This time, the 'way' manifested in the form of shortening the distance between the two of us by almost a 1000 km, by a shift of our residence from Delhi to Goa. My father had accepted an offer to serve as chief engineer with the state electricity department of the spectacular land of churches and beaches. Anyhow, before I continue with the account of my 'pen love affair', I can't refrain from straying for a while to take you through the overwhelming memories of our relocation.

My heart and spirit frisked with delight at the forthcoming proposition of going to the most beautiful part of the country. The excitement was intense; I could scarcely wait to be amidst the glorious palm trees clustering upon the golden sands of the beaches fringing the vast blue Arabian Sea. This would be my very first meeting with the ocean, and in addition, Goa was well known for its dance and music. Therefore, I was now totally immersed in the wonderful prospect of new people, new food, new places, and an entirely new culture. On one cold January morning, we boarded the train for Bombay and were on our way. On the train, I recall our peeling off our woolens as we approached the city of Bombay, and the uncomfortably hot and humid weather of the legendary city.

A very tall and hefty gentleman bearing the name, Ashok Bhovay, who had been deputed to receive us at Bombay and to escort us to a suitable place to spend a couple of days, met us at the Bombay station. He proved to be a friendly and jolly Goan, who had a host of equally hospitable relatives and friends in the city. We stayed at one of his uncle's small apartment in the heart of the city, while Bhovay himself went on to Goa to prepare for our reception. With so much to see and so much to do, the two days that we were in Bombay simply zipped by. I for one, did not take to the city very much: there was too much traffic, and too many people rushing around, and the heat and humidity was painful. This was already casting a shadow over the blissful anticipation that had accompanied me from Delhi: 'Would Goa be like this,' I pondered, 'and if so, I have my reservations about the seaside'.

7 a.m. of the third morning at Bombay saw us aboard the small steamer docked on a dirty, smelly, and extremely noisy jetty. Apprehension and curiosity tugging at my heart, when I, along with my family, embarked the ready to sail vessel via a shaky wooden ramp on to the lower decks. It was fearfully gloomy and suffocating in there. Picking our way through a mass of unruly, sweating voyagers and heaps of bags and bundles, we arrived at the bottom of a rickety wooden ladder, which took us to the middle deck. Here too, we were to engage in further wrestles with the ever-growing multitude till we eventually reached the upper deck where our cabins were located.

Then, as I stepped out on to the open walkway leading to our cabins, the fresh morning air and sunlight somewhat restored my dampening spirits. We had been booked into two first class cabins. Each of these had two bunk beds neatly covered with crisp bed linen and soft blankets on either side of the cabin, with a tiny washroom at the far side. It all felt very cozy and peaceful in there. Sandy and I shared a cabin and my parents settled into the other one.

Tucking my handbag into the small closet under the bunk, Sandy and I cautiously stepped out into the corridor to further explore the tiny liner in which we were to sail.

This was to be our maiden cruise, and I had in fact never set my eyes upon a real ship before. Therefore, now that we were actually on board, all ready to sail, excitement took over. All the passengers stood waving and watching over the rails as the steamer hooted its farewell and gradually glided away from the jetty. Soon, our steamer reached the open waters of the Arabian Sea on its 24-hour voyage to Goa. Although the shore was nearly always in view from one side of the steamer, the thrill of being astride such a powerful vastness of water made my heart skip many a beat. I am ever so grateful to the Almighty to have left me with sufficient eyesight to be able to witness and capture in my memory, the vivid panorama stretched out before me. The green-blue dancing waves glittering in the bright golden sunlight, with the sparkling silvery white foam in the wake of the craft was an unforgettable extravaganza. I spent the entire day gazing transfixed to the enchantment, soaking in the display that Mother Nature was holding out for my gaze.

The spectacle had entirely engulfed me with its charm, leaving room for only a few recollections, other than those of the dazzling environment spread around. The fragrance of the sea had now totally overpowered the unpleasant pungent odour of rotting fish, and the soft hum of the boat engine, and the melodic lapping of waves in the breeze replaced the ear-shattering noise of the shrieking crowds. Only too soon for my taste, the glorious colours of the day melted into the pitch darkness of night. Then, as I stood staring into the profound darkness, the moon decided to appear in its divine majesty, and leave its shimmering reflection upon the black waters, imprinted forever upon the canvas of my memory.

Early next morning, we arrived at the small Panjim (Panaji now) harbour, the capital of Goa, and, our arrival there on another smelly, noisy, and overcrowded jetty brought back the sinking feeling I had left behind at the Bombay harbour. The atmosphere of this dock too gave me the creeps; my dreams once more crumbled, and deep disappointment loomed. Where was the land as beautiful as a picture postcard? I was constantly covering my nose with all available articles to prevent myself from throwing up in the prevailing stench, as I reluctantly trudged through the slippery slush on the walkway to the waiting car. Everything smelt of rotting fish. Where were the golden beaches, palm trees, and 'blue sea' I had heard so much about? All I could see were heaps of rotting rubbish thrown in and around collapsing garbage enclosures, and to top it all, we were taken directly to a dingy and crammed government colony to an equally spooky apartment for breakfast.

'Is this Goa?' Sandy and I cried in unison, 'We were better off in Delhi! Wish we had never come here…'

Now however, the damage was done; we were already here and had no choice. Therefore, with an effort, we mustered our best manners and put on a phony delighted expression when Mr and Mrs D.L. Gulati and their three children very warmly welcomed us to their home. The Gulatis had been friends of my parents from old times in Simla, and Mr. Gulati and my father were also colleagues. Sanjeev, their eldest son, Vikki, the second, and Ruby, their little daughter, together gave us their not overly encouraging account of Goa. They had already been here for over a year and had found nothing particularly special or exciting; on the contrary, they felt that north Indians were not very welcomed in this coastal land. This was not at all encouraging for our already slumped spirits; the smile completely disappeared from my lips and a heavy weight settled within my heart. Sandy at least had a friendship in the offing as Sanjeev was his age, but for me, there only seemed to be a vacuum.

We spent much of the day at the Gulati's residence, and after a sumptuous lunch of *rajma* and rice, we were escorted to the government circuit house at Altino. Then, as we stepped out of the car in front of the circuit house, our disappointment evaporated into thin air; the place was breathtakingly beautiful, with clean, good roads lined on both sides by lush green trees, and no fishy smell whatsoever.

We were allotted two rooms on the first floor of the lofty old edifice furnished with scanty traditional furniture. As it was late evening, we settled our luggage into these rooms and went down to the empty dining room for our evening meal. A rickety old waiter soon appeared from somewhere and inquired what we would like for dinner. 'Do you serve fish here?' we inquired, looking forward to our first Goan meal. He nodded his 'fishy' bald head with long whiskers sticking out of his ears, and disappeared into the kitchen to return with two dishes of brown watery curry and rice. Greedily, we ploughed into the dishes and found a few tiny bits of some meat, which he assured us, were the fish. Anyhow, we were hungry and as we had no alternate arrangement for dinner, we made the most of the fish curry and rice on our table.

Post-dinner, we trudged back to our respective rooms and turned in for the night. As was the practice, Sandy and I shared a room and Mummy and Daddy took the room across the corridor. With the lights turned off, the room seemed quite spooky with its high ceiling and wobbly wooden beds with an equally rattling mosquito net frames over each of the beds. Sleep soon took over and then suddenly, I was startled out of my sleep by Sandy jumping up and down violently in the narrow space between our two beds! 'Snake... snake...,' he screamed at the top of his lungs. 'Get them off... kill them... hurry... help... help,' he kept shouting, 'bring me a stick... quick... they are all wrapped around my legs...' he screamed, getting wilder and wilder.

With my heart in my mouth and not being able to see anything, I, for a moment pictured hundreds of snakes attacking my poor brother. Panic-stricken, standing on the bed, I tried to pull him on to mine, but without any success. Instead, his jumping and screaming became even louder. 'Why did we have to come to this godforsaken place?' I groaned, 'what do I do now?'

Then, as suddenly as it had erupted, Sandy's crazy act stopped; sitting down on his bed, rubbing his eyes, he inquired in surprise, 'What is the matter? Why are you standing up on your bed?' Then, a little shakily, he went on, 'But good you woke me up; I was dreaming of snakes wrapped around my legs.' I could have hit him. I was half out of my mind with fright and shock; and he says he was dreaming. Well, I pushed him off into his bed and lay down to get back to sleep myself, but after this crazy episode, it proved futile.

We were required to vacate the circuit house in ten days' time and as the house in the electricity colony where we were to live was still occupied by the outgoing chief engineer; we were allotted a small temporary apartment on the other side of Altinho hill. This was a shabby, dingy ground floor flat with a tiny balcony outside the small kitchen. Indeed, if one dared to step out on to the little ledge for want of fresh air, you would be adorned either with trash, or dirty water from the kitchens above! When we asked the cleaning woman about this, she informed us gloomily, 'Throwing everything out of the kitchen window is the law of the land in these parts, either you stay indoors or like me, be prepared for all kinds of things to land on your head.' Equipped with this piece of valuable information, we cordoned off the balcony for the three months we lived in the house.

With nothing much to do during the day, I decided to utilize the period to get some of the ugly fat off my back. I therefore ate boiled vegetables, took morning and evening walks, used a skipping rope, and followed the Canadian Air Force Exercise routine, and mopped and dusted the house, all of which had a beneficial effect on my waistline. When we moved to the colony bungalow, I was 15 kg lighter, with a figure many may have envied!

By then, Sandy had joined school and Daddy was wholly immersed in his challenging responsibilities, while Mummy and I busied ourselves doing up our new home.

Our house was quite spacious, with a large front door and two large windows overlooking the long but narrow front verandah. On the ground wall, there were drawing and dining rooms, two lobbies, and a large kitchen. The outer door of the kitchen led on to another veranda extending to the back of the house, with a view of the very large kitchen garden, and the gorgeous sun setting into the shimmering sea. Strange as it may sound, I am still not certain whether I ever actually saw the setting sun or whether it was my mother's graphic description of the scene that the vivid picture of the glowing orange sun drowning in the glittering mass of water that was imprinted on my mind.

From the central lobby, a wide red staircase majestically led to the first floor landing which was surrounded by the three large bedrooms, one bathroom, and a large terrace. Two of the bedrooms had little private balconies and were therefore chosen by Sandy and me as our rooms; and our parents occupied the third. The servant's quarter behind the kitchen was home to Bilkis, our housemaid, and her three children. The drive-in garage, connected to the main house through the ground floor inner lobby, and the pretty front lawn splashed with flowers and bordered by a massive wood rose creeper, added to the elegance of the building.

In no time at all, we settled into this luxurious house and fell into step with life in the captivating state of Goa. My days were overflowing with activities like writing profusely to my pen boyfriend, reading his replies over and over again, and immersing myself into any book I could get hold of. Planning and cooking the midday meal was my responsibility, and in addition, I had to make time for exercising, walking, and going swimming.

Socializing was extremely popular in this small city, and before long, both Sandy and I had loads of friends in and out of the house. My father was nominated as an honorary member of the army mess, which gave us the opportunity to attend most of their social events like the weekly tambola session and film shows, followed by dinner. In addition, the army campus housed one of the most exquisite swimming pools, tiled with beautifully designed antique Portuguese tiles, so swimming became a part of our daily routine.

With the acquisition of our first music system, evenings turned into an energetic jam session in our drawing room. All it required was to turn up the volume of the record player and from nowhere would appear Cheekoo, David, Nirmal, and Atul, and off went the coffee table and small carpet, and the dancing would commence to the gay rocking melodies of the Beatles, Carpenters, and the Teens. Then heaven alone knows how the arrival of Sheela, Nancy, and Sonia would instantly spice up the party even further. Usually, the inevitable appearance of Atul's mother on her 'son-hunting' spree brought the mini jam session to a stop for the evening. My parents never seemed to object seeing us both having a good time, and they would go off to visit their own friends, busied themselves with shopping, or simply enjoyed the garden.

The initial disappointment of Goa had been long forgotten; we were now merrily plunging into making the most of the exclusive, luxurious vacation with the round the clock entertainment it provided. Picnics on the most spectacular beaches in the world was a customary way to pass time; splashing among the gentle waves and collecting shells from the unsoiled sandy shores was the most natural thing to do.

Witnessing the famous three-day Carnival of Goa before the commencement of the month-long Lent fasting was in itself an amazing experience. I had never seen something so gay and cheerful; it was really thrilling to see processions of hundreds of people dancing in the streets accompanied by an array of bands playing atop brilliantly decorated trucks. Then, there were the all night dances organized right on the streets on all the three nights of the celebration. On our first carnival in Goa, we went to one of these dances on the final night and danced off our feet to the mesmerizing music played by the live band. The fun seemed to last forever, until a strange jarring sound heard above the blaring band, startled me. I stopped in my tracks and asked Raymond, my dancing partner, 'Hey, what is wrong with the music?' 'Nothing,' he replied, with a puzzled smile. Ignoring his answer, and even more surprised as the sound was growing louder, I asked again whether something had gone wrong with the speakers. 'Can't you hear it, Raymond; can't you hear the loud funny sound,' I insisted. Then suddenly he broke out laughing, 'Oh silly woman,' he blurted out, shaking me by the shoulders, 'it's the crows! It is morning now and they have to wake up, don't they?' 'It can't be morning already! That does not sound anything like crows at all to me,' I protested, 'I know what crows sound like, and so don't try to fool me just because I am new to Goa!'

Later, however, when the dancing eventually came to an end and we were going home, I really found out for myself that the sound was actually from the crows. Goa was home to millions of crows, and thankfully so, for how else would Mother Nature clean up the tons of rotting fish thrown on the shore by the fisher folk. My dear crows are truly responsible for keeping the golden sandy beaches as clean as they are; and also for the smelly blotches of digested fish on your head, in the event of your omitting to unfurl your umbrella when taking an evening walk in the tree-lined streets near the shore. Interestingly, ever since, I have loved the hardworking black bird dearly, and as we go along in this tale, you will see how they played a central role in whatever I have been able to achieve today.

One fine mid-morning, I scooped up my 'pen boyfriend's' letter from the lobby floor, raced up the stately stairway, humming happily, to lap up the contents of the love letter in the seclusion of my bedroom. 'I am coming to Goa to see you my darling…' were the words that greeted my magical magnifying glasses. I read the line over and over again, just to ensure I was not dreaming. Tucking the letter away into the large cardboard packaging of a five liter bottle of Balantyne Scotch Whisky (which I used for storing 'love letters'), I went in search of Mummy.

'Mummy… oh mummy,' I cried, as I tore around the house at top speed; 'Narandra is coming to Goa next week.' 'And where is he going to stay?' she inquired, trying to keep the concern out of her voice. 'Oh, here with us of course; he is coming to spend time with me and so here is where he will be,' I responded gaily. 'But, well,' she muttered doubtfully; then after a moment, she went on, 'OK, I think it should be fine to put him up here. I will have to ask your father's permission.' I was delighted with her approval and knew with certainty that as she had given the green signal, Daddy would not object. There was complete trust and harmony between my parents and I had never ever to this day seen them disagreeing, let alone quarreling.

I went around all excited and charged; my doctor boyfriend was after all coming the extra hundreds of miles just to see me. This appeared promising, and in my heart, I had identified him as my much longed for life partner.

On the appointed day, I stood waiting for my heartthrob on the front verandah, expecting him to alight from each passing car. At last, the much awaited taxi arrived and Mummy proclaimed, 'I think this is him.' Struggling for composure and disguising my nervous shyness, I walked down the three steps of the verandah and up the garden path to greet him. Shaking his hand warmly, I introduced myself and was disappointed at his 'south Indian mixed with Hindustani' English accent, as well as the monotonous tone of voice as he did the same. My heart fell further when I sensed his medium height, his excessively meek and insipid manner and paucity of sophistication.

My well-bred upbringing instantly came to my rescue and I heard myself saying politely, 'Please do come on in Narandra, I am so pleased you could come,' a complete white lie. 'Hope you had a comfortable journey?'

As soon as Narandra went upstairs to freshen up, my mother quickly gave me an update on my new boyfriend. 'Your friend is not very tall,' she commented smiling, 'and he is not very fair either.' I listened with a bothered look as she went on, 'but he looks intelligent and perhaps you can polish him up a bit later.' Crestfallen and further disheartened by Mummy's opinion of my boyfriend, yet not wishing to overlook the prospect of having found my soul-mate, I decided to get motivated. 'He does not seem so bad after all, and anyhow, he is a doctor, which is more than I can ask for,' I told myself. 'And anyway, I won't wear high heels after marriage and once he begins working in the US, the polish will come on its own accord.' Thus reconciled, I decided to make the most of what I had at the present and cheered myself further with phrases like, 'one can't ask for every thing' and 'I too have my negative points.' Thus, casting off any negative feelings and thoughts from my mind, I truly enjoyed my pen pal boyfriend's visit. Though we spent most of the time chatting about virtually everything under the sun, sadly no offer of marriage was forthcoming. I did force some silly love talk at times, but thankfully, it got nowhere! However, what really gave me the most pleasure were the perfumes, soaps, shampoos, and the pink sari he brought from America. To this day, I wonder what made him bring me a clothes iron too!

Well, following the departure of my special visitor, life promptly swung back to normal. There was not much time for me to fret, and no inclination either to miss the gentleman, for the meeting in person had taken the shine off the affair. Perhaps when the time did come for marriage, he might be the one I would marry, provided I did not find a better match.

In the time being, I got dragged deeper and deeper into the exhilarating lifestyle of Goa. There were so many attractive young men around that Narandra soon faded into the background. Letters went back and forth between us, but the fervour was missing. However, sometime later, a letter from him announced his plan to move to the US, so, simply out of curiosity, I asked him about the future of our relationship. Back came his reply: 'Well, I am not sure,' he wrote, 'whenever my father brings up the matter of my marriage, I will definitely suggest your name, and if he approves of you, I will definitely marry you!'

I was absolutely livid and very hurt by this conceited comment and his audacity to dare to thoughtlessly display such a shallow mindset towards the girl he claimed to love so very much. I immediately pulled out my little typewriter and wrote back in a fury, plainly telling him that I was not in the least bit interested in getting married to him. 'Please return all the photographs you have of me by return of post and do not bother to ever again write to me,' I thumped out.

Back came my photographs in a couple of days and a small note from him expressing his regret at the sudden break of this wonderful relationship.

Relieved at having him off my back, I tore up the hundred odd love letters and disposed of the shreds along with the unsuccessful association into the bin! Then I sang and danced away my failure to the words of a motivating *Kirtan*, a particular devotional song from the Guru Granth Sahib, which gave me the courage to live up to the will of God. I realized that this particular experience had helped me to develop, and now I was free to hope for better things to come my way. Ever since that afternoon, I have never regretted the break-up.

As luck would have it, a proposal for marriage for me arrived through a relative in Chandigarh, filling my empty, romance-deprived heart with a ray of hope. The prospective bridegroom was a Sikh air force officer who was looking for a second wife after his first had left him for reasons unknown! He was ready to marry me notwithstanding my disability. This was very good news for my entire family, although my parents were not at all certain about the idea. However, in the face of repeated assurances and cajoling on the part of the relatives, they decided to take a closer look at the proposition and prepared to make an unscheduled trip to Punjab to meet the gentleman concerned.

When my mother informed me about this, I was not particularly enthused with the arrangement as for one thing; the gentleman had a proper turban and beard, which anyway disqualified him from achieving my professed criteria of a husband. However, after assessing the pros and cons of my situation in relation to matrimony, I too began to view the proposal in a somewhat favourable light. If I took an honest look at the present state of affairs, there were not many men who would readily marry a blind girl. I therefore resorted to my well-practiced self motivation technique of picking out the positive points from any given situation, and thereafter, adhering wholeheartedly to them.

So it was that even before we left Goa on this eventful journey, I had self-talked myself into falling in love with this man, and when on our arrival in Delhi I learnt that there was no question of any doubts as to the success of the proposal, I was secretly thrilled. The prospective bridegroom wished to have the wedding within the following fortnight as he had liked me very much from the photograph of me he had seen, and of course, my family could not have been better placed.

Daddy had not accompanied us when we left Goa, as nothing very urgent was planned or known. We had been informed that this was only a trip to enable us to meet; if all went well, the wedding would be scheduled a few months hence. Curiously, however, matters had suddenly taken an unexpected turn and, it was decided that the moment all of us had consented to the match following the proposed meeting in Chandigarh, Daddy would fly in for the wedding.

The following afternoon, we were in Chandigarh and I was almost beside myself with sweet dreams of my new life: a caring husband, and a home of my own. Ecstasy was the name of my game with wedding bells around the corner. 'He must be a truly wonderful human being,' I thought, 'a man who could, just like that, without even knowing me, be willing to marry me, fully aware of my disability, had to be wonderful.' Who ever said there weren't good and noble men in our community?

'Now I must quickly plan out what I want in my wedding hamper,' I thought. 'I think my preference is for traditional saris in bright and fresh colours. Oh, and I have to list out all the stuff I will need for my home. I must buy an oven and a washing machine,' I told myself, my thoughts running away with me. 'I think we will go tomorrow morning to Sector 17 and Daddy can bring the saris that Mummy has already bought for me. I hope he does not forget the beautiful green one with the magenta border that, I think, is lying in my cupboard and not with the rest of them. And of course... the jewellery... Mummy can give me some...' and then, my rushing thoughts were jolted to a complete halt by raised voices from the dining table where my grandparents and mother were finishing their lunch. 'How is this possible,' my grandmother said sharply, 'then why was the information not given to you people yesterday when you were in Delhi?'

With a sinking feeling in my stomach, I joined the elders at the table to find out the cause for the sudden uproar and commotion. You can imagine my shock when I heard the news that my so-called prospective bridegroom was at the time on his way to marry another woman in Patiala. It felt as if someone had slapped me full in my face. I had never known any pain as intense, as unbearable, like this crashing dream and breaking of heart. Despair, dejection, and deep hurt and disappointment engulfed my entire being. I tried to appear unperturbed, which I succeeded in doing most successfully, but my soul bled with pain, hopelessness, and depression threatened to shatter my spirit completely.

We spent a few weeks in Chandigarh, but I have no recollection of what went on around me, except that I wanted to give up. 'Why God,' I demanded to know over and over again, 'why does this happen to me? I never asked this guy to marry me; then why did he have to volunteer? Why did he have to divorce me from a perfectly happy life when he had intended to marry someone else? Why did this entire drama have to occur when I was not at all keen to marry him in the first place... It was only his genuine apparent kindness that had touched my heart and I had made up my mind to accept his generosity. And then why, when I had eventually become so deeply attached to him, had fate so completely and cruelly dashed my hopes. Hadn't I already suffered sufficiently; been tossed and battered mercilessly through life's toughest punishments at so young an age? I don't think this is fair, God; I can't take it any more.' These thoughts went round and round in my head; I wept bitterly but silently through the nights, lest anyone learn of my deep affliction. I was aware that my parents too were feeling wretched about the whole affair and I did not want to add to their pain with my own. I therefore went about my day, smiling and acting normal when with them; and ever so often shut myself in the bathroom to spill the threatening tears and emerged dry-eyed and smiling once more.

It has been almost over thirty years since I went through this dreadful experience, but even as I write about it today, I realize that even now its memory evokes a sharp pain from somewhere deep within. Even today, deep within me, lays a wish to reveal to these callous people the damage they inflicted, of the spirit they so cruelly scarred. Very seldom do people realize even momentarily what their words and actions may result in for others around. However, as I write this narrative, I am grateful to God for having taken me through these types of experiences because they taught me to think before acting or speaking. I learnt too that I should put myself into others' shoes before saying or doing anything, lest my words or actions cause them the slightest pain. This notwithstanding, there have however been occasions, when I have not been able to please everyone, no matter how hard I tried, even at the cost of my own happiness.

Well, anyhow, our return home very rapidly dulled the sting of this tragedy; the blue green waves lapping with unending strength and unfailing persistence upon the golden sands gave me the courage to get on with life again. The possibility of better luck in the future was still there, and the man with long hair and beard was not, after all, to be lived with... the affair had after all fizzled out, and I was free to love again. To hope once more of finding the life partner of my dreams; the man who would love me more than his life... I had to reach out for the man for whom I would be his world. I knew in my bones and believed with my entire being that such a man was somewhere out there... and if not yet, God had to create him for me, for I would not rest till I found him. I was willing to pay the price, which I somehow knew would be tremendous, but even the greatest price would be worth paying for the man I dreamt of because the life 'he' would give me would be priceless. Whatever happened was for the best, I told myself, and plunged right into the music, dancing, and general merriment that Goa had to offer.

⠉⠋

'Would you like to work in our hotel?' asked a voice from across the dining table at a dinner party in the Fidalgo Resort. Wondering if the question was addressed to me, I looked in the direction of the voice, 'would you, Preeti?'

Excited and surprised, I happily nodded my acceptance. Then, addressing my father, 'Why don't you bring her along to my office tomorrow morning and let her join,' said the general manager of a five star hotel.

Sleep refused to be my guest that night; I was up with the first 'caw' of my dear friend, the crow. Cheerfully but a bit nervously, I dressed in my green and red floral printed chiffon sari. My hands trembled with anticipation as I brushed my hair and with difficulty, swallowed breakfast; then clutching at my red handbag, I settled myself into my father's office car to be dropped off at the hotel for my first job.

I spent two very happy days at the hotel getting inducted into the house-keeping department. Then, on the second evening, we had a surprise visit from the GM of the hotel; he was there to apologetically ask my parents not to send me to the hotel any more. The employees of the hotel had gone on a strike due to my ad-hoc appointment.

This was most shocking! What had I done now? Was I so bad that no one, no one at all wished to have anything to do with me? First it was my school, then the music teacher's denial that I would be able to achieve excellence no matter how hard I worked. No one seemed to want to marry me and now hundreds of people were protesting just because I had dared to accept a humble trainee's position at a five star hotel. This seemed too absurd to make any sense of; just because I was blind, I was apparently being denied the basic right to live in this world.

Once more, I was beset with sadness, over and over again my efforts to survive as a human being were being swept away. The foot I extended to walk along with the rest would ruthlessly be kicked off its foothold, as if to say, 'You blind girl, be thankful for our sympathy; do not attempt to walk our paths, and if you don't desist, we'll stop you in your tracks by one means or another.' 'This was as much my world as theirs,' I would think, 'then why was I not being allowed to do what I was doing? I was not snatching anything from anyone, I meant no harm, and only wished to live with dignity. Where do I go, to be able to simply live life like everyone else? How could I bring back the diminishing light into my eyes, when there was no cure anywhere in the world? I worked harder than most, suffered years of painful and harsh treatment of every variety just in order to be able to play my part like any other citizen of the world. I took great pains to learn to do everything other people did, even though I had to work a thousand times harder than them; and endure far greater hardships, but I was now a highly accomplished young girl! Cooking, knitting, housekeeping… I could do it all and possessed excellent social skills. I could swim, read, and write, and could also hold an intelligent conversation with anyone, and yet, according to able-bodied people, I was no good! No one wanted to share this world with me! Why?'

Assailed by such thoughts, and vowing to keep learning whatever I chanced upon, I resolved never to give up. 'I don't care what people say, I'm going to live a happy life anyhow,' became my motto. When I had my friends and family adoring and admiring me, I had simply no reason or excuse to sit around moping and making myself and those around me who were my loving strengths, miserable.

I therefore returned to dancing and roaming the cool streets and beaches of Goa with the most desirable young people in town, and made the most of every available opportunity that came my way. Before I move on to the next images, I must tell you of the way God not only repairs the damaged hearts of His children, but makes them look and feel a thousand times better than they were before the inflictions.

We were at the New Year Eve dance in the winter of 1979, waiting for the midnight special dance to begin. I stood with a couple of my girlfriends on the pavement next to the makeshift dance floor on the street in the heart of Panjim, wondering whether I would have the good fortune of finding my dream dance partner. Each time a young man walked up to our group, I hoped I was going to be asked for the midnight dance, but all in vain. My smile shrunk and my enthusiasm dipped with every passing minute. 'It is true, I am no good, and no one even wishes to dance with me,' when my thoughts were interrupted by the gentle touch of a hand on my shoulder, followed by the deep voice of Melvin whispering into my ear, 'Hey Penny, you are booked for the midnight special, OK?' The smile flashed back, my fallen self-esteem and confidence soared; I felt like the princess of the world. I, having been asked to dance the 'midnight special' by the most eligible and sought after bachelor in our friend circle. 'I am the best!' I told myself to prop up my drooping spirits.

I even decided to try my hand at writing. I wrote a seventeen-page romantic story and sent it to *Femina* for publication. The inevitable obviously happened: they sent it right back with a note that said: Sorry, we will not be able to publish this story because it does not fall within our mandate. I shred the story into pieces and flung it into the bin, swearing to myself that one day my work would be published.

You know, this was not the first occasion that my writing had found a place in the bin; my class teacher once flung my English language notebook into the class wastepaper basket across the classroom in full view of all the forty-five students, after having angrily crossed out the essay I had written. 'This is unacceptable Preeti,' she screamed at the already self-conscious and scared twelve-year-old, 'After all that I have taught, you can't even write one correct sentence!' I was of course heartbroken then, and I have never forgotten the humiliation to which I was subjected and probably somewhere deep in my heart, my sufferings were being converted into the foundations of a better tomorrow.

For the moment, no further adversity of any significance beset me, and the summer of 1980 saw us bid farewell to the magnificent land of Goa. Back in Delhi, we this time moved into an apartment in Sector 8 of the same government colony. Though this apartment had five rooms, a kitchen plus a bathroom with a little balcony, it felt like a matchbox compared to the bungalow in Goa.

Before continuing with the story of my life, I must tell you that tiny Chicki, a beautiful white spitz, had joined our family in Goa. Chicki had come as a birthday present for Sandy from a neighbour there, and was now the beloved of us all.

Having moved into a new neighbourhood, it was going to take us some time to settle in. With Sandy preoccupied with his studies and Daddy with his work, Mummy and I grew closer to each other. We shared the household chores, went vegetable shopping, and visited neighbours to make new acquaintances together.

Though I would still spend a lot of my time reading and writing, I would make it a point to listen to Mummy read the Guru Granth Sahab every day. I listened to the verses attentively, trying to understand the scripture. Mummy too would explain the meanings of the scripture a little at a time, and I gradually became deeply interested in what I learnt. Something within nudged me not only to just listen, but also practice what the holy book preached.

At about this time, we heard about the National Open School, a special distance learning institution for school dropouts. My parents were very keen that I acquire some formal education and they succeeded in convincing me that I should study for the class 10 examinations via the NOS. Although, this idea did not attract me, this time I gave in to my parent's wishes.

I was also taken to the Blind Relief Association (BRA), a school for blind boys, to see whether I could learn a vocation. The principal, himself blind, advised me to learn braille to enable me to read and write independently. I agreed to this, and began my tuition in the script for the blind.

It was tough for my mother, as it was a 20-minute walk to the bus stop and then a bus ride of almost over an hour, and thereafter, she had to wait for a couple of hours for my lesson to be over. So while I took my lessons, Mummy utilized her time reading to the blind students in the school.

During this time, we encountered a number of blind people working for the betterment of the blind, and most of them disapproved of the way I had been brought up. In any event, neither my parents nor I shared that view, especially after seeing the condition of the blind students all around us, I was far better off than any of them. Yes, they did have a formal education as far as books and certificates were concerned, but everything else was missing. On the other hand, I had acquired an excellent personality, very good communication skills, and a great amount of general knowledge, along with excellent survival skills. I had lived in mainstream society and was perfectly capable of conducting myself in any given situation without evoking too much pity or unnecessary alarm. Usually, not many people guessed that I was blind, and instead wondered why I acted somewhat strangely in doing certain things. For example, I had earned the reputation of being a snob, as I never responded to silent smiles and salutations, little realizing that I could not see what they were doing.

I usually took little Chicki for short walks around our block and would generally run down the two floors on my own to the scooter garage to fetch letters. I would be seen putting out the washing on the line and also looked quite cheerful washing or mopping the balcony on days when our maid failed to turn up. 'How could she be blind?' they must all have wondered, 'she does not look blind.'

The young people living in our block were probably too involved with their own lives to pay me any attention, I reckoned. Interestingly, once I got talking to a young man from the apartment above ours, and a few weeks later, his mom told me to keep out of his way. 'You see,' I recall her telling me, 'we are Bengali Brahmins and it will not be possible for us to accept you as our daughter-in-law.' I guess it was too dangerous for a young man to even so much as get friendly with this blind girl; she might just trick him into marrying her. Did I present such a threat? But quite honestly, it did hurt me after all.

Then one day, my grandfather called my father and informed him that he had advertised in the matrimonial section of the *Sunday* newspaper for me. 'I have not mentioned her handicap,' he said, 'in this way, we will attract a sizable number of suitors for Penny; and if you so wish, we can inform those who come over to see her.' My father was not at all pleased with this, but now he was not left with any alternative but to go along with it. Following this, we had all kinds of people visiting our home to examine me. Thankfully, I never had to go on display, but it was certainly a nerve shattering experience to watch prospective grooms and their relatives sprint out of our home when they learnt of my impaired vision. There were none who mustered the 'courage' or courtsey to so much as meet me. It also became rather comical, when one of them, in his haste to escape from me, rushed to exit our home via the window rather than the door, and the irony was that this prospective groom himself walked with a limp.

The issue of my marriage was becoming a nightmare, and was blown out of proportion by everyone. Thank heavens my parents had a very different outlook towards the matter, which kept me sane and in a reasonably positive frame of mind throughout these demoralizing happenings. I wondered why the world around was leaving no stone unturned to see me married so that I would be off my parents' head.

I was just about twenty-one, but it seemed that I was committing a cardinal sin in still remaining single, and in my parental home. This was of course taking a toll on me too, and I was rapidly beginning to believe that I had become the source of immense unhappiness to my close family. My own efforts to find a life partner were also proving to be singularly unsuccessful. I know my parents, especially my mother, suffered along with me, as like any other mother, she too wished for her daughter's happiness and well-being, which meant finding a husband. But where was he to be found?

One thing which I was still very certain about was that my spirit was much too willful to be bound down to a compromise; and that too for the remainder of my life. No matter what people thought or said, I just could not go ahead and marry anyone who was prepared to take me for his wife. I had at least to like the man who I was going to marry. It was not much to ask for a good person with good values and a humane outlook. Other attributes had ceased to matter by then, but where was I to find such a man? I had looked and was still in the process of doing so, as I myself did not wish to remain a spinster forever. Therefore, I lived every day as it came, trying to keep busy with things that I enjoyed, while keeping a watchful eye for Mr Right to make an appearance.

Days passed relatively uneventfully, while we eagerly awaited Sandy's class twelfth results. Then on 28 May 1982, the day for celebration arrived. It was late afternoon when we received the wonderful news that Sandy had passed out from school, and both he and Mummy went out to the market to buy sweets before Daddy returned from office.

A few minutes after they left, the doorbell rang. Thinking it was my father, I enthusiastically hurried to let him in and be the first one to convey the fantastic news. So, without asking who it was, I flung open the door and was about to blurt out the good news, when I was stopped in mid-sentence by a deep male voice asking, 'Is Sandy home?'

Disappointed at not finding my father at the door, and somewhat surprised to see a stranger instead, I stood inquiringly in the open doorway, wondering who this was. 'Is Sandy in?' asked the stranger once more, in a deep masculine voice.

'Well,' I said, 'No, he has gone to the market.' 'OK, never mind,' came the very polite reply, 'I will come later.' Normally when I was alone at home, I refrained from inviting in strangers, but on this occasion, something made me do just that. To this he responded politely, 'I will return after a while, please don't bother.' With that, he was gone, leaving me speculating at the wide-open doorway, where Daddy found me minutes later. His 'Hello dear' jerked me back to the present, and Daddy asked, 'have you been waiting for me?' Collecting my thoughts quickly, I congratulated him for his son's results and we were still chattering excitedly when Sandy and Mummy returned, and the celebrations began in earnest.

A short while later, the doorbell sounded; it was John, Sandy's friend, who was here to congratulate him. This was the first time I was meeting John, and the three of us sat chatting at the dining table, when the doorbell announced the next visitor.

My father opened the door this time and in a moment, I heard the same deep and polished voice ask for Sandy. And immediately afterwards, the owner of the fascinating voice and manner was standing beside the table, heartily congratulating Sandy. 'I am Keith,' he said, introducing himself, 'I am John's elder brother and I thought I would take this opportunity to come and meet you guys.'

From that day onwards, Keith became a regular visitor to our home. Sandy or no Sandy, he was at our house every other day, and then every day. I was completely taken over by his personality, manners, and his fantastic talents. He could sing my favourite songs, play the guitar, was a superb cook, ran all manners of errands, and most of all, was extremely dependable. On top of all this, Keith was very good looking with straight brown hair and lively grey-green eyes.

Before I realized what was happening, I was completely captivated; I had fallen madly in love with this amazing Anglo-Indian youth! What else could I have asked for; this time it was not one-sided; he reciprocated my love in equal measure. I had never before experienced such care, such kindness, so much benevolence, and utter devotion from a young man. My disability was of no consequence; he loved me for what I was and hadn't ever known a family as simple and loving as ours, and wished for nothing more in the world than to be a part of it.

It was as if my lifelong prayers had been answered in the form of this man; God was after all great! The Lord had not allowed any other man to claim my hand, explaining the innumerable rejections I had been subjected to, because he had intended this very special man for me.

Keith worked for a publishing house, was very God-fearing and often assured me, 'You need not bother about anything; I will look after the house, the children, and bring in the money as well.' It was not long before he asked me to marry him, and I was more than happy to accept. When Keith informed his parents of our wedding plans, most unexpectedly they immediately responded in the negative. 'She is not a Catholic, and besides, she is blind,' they protested. As Keith had decided to go ahead with his wedding plans anyhow, he moved out of his parents' home into a one room rented apartment in a nearby colony. This provided me additional assurance of his intentions and strengthened my trust in him. As it was to be an inter-religion marriage, we decided to have a registered marriage at the earliest. So on 1 October 1982, we put in our application for a court marriage. We now could be legally married after exactly thirty days of the application and our wedding day was fixed for 1 November.

Although I was in the process of listing out the things that I would need for my new little home, Keith now felt that it would be difficult for me to live with him on our own. Even after repeated assurances regarding my capacity to manage extremely well, he requested my parents to permit us to live in with them after marriage; to which they happily consented. I personally was not very happy with this arrangement because I wanted a home of my own, and also did not wish to place a further burden upon my parents and brother. Once everything had been fixed up, Keith virtually moved in with us; going over to his tiny room for a few hours each week simply to have a look at the few belongings he had left there.

Then, some weeks later, Keith left our house for his office at the usual time, saying he would be back home by 7.00 p.m. that evening. He usually called me once during the day, but on this particular day, I didn't hear from him at all, so I called his office just to say 'Hello'. His boss answered my call and when I asked for Keith, I was told that he had not been coming to work for the last three days. Alarmed, worried, and confused, I thanked him, not knowing what to make of it. Keith had religiously been going to work every day; at least that is where he had said he had been going to each morning. Even if he was unwell, he should have rested at home rather than lying to me, and if he was not unwell and had been attending office, then why should his boss lie to me? There was something seriously wrong with this whole affair. Also, if Keith was lying to me now, I knew for certain, he would always continue to do the same.

Shaken, and utterly shattered, all I could think of was that nothing had happened so far: we were not yet married and therefore I must act right away. How could I live with someone who was being dishonest with me? How would I ever in the future be able to trust him? These doubts were sufficient to make me decide to call off our wedding.

My mother had gone off for the day to my grandparents' home and my father was at work. Too upset by my discovery, I rang up my mother and told her what had happened. 'I don't want to marry him Mummy,' I wept. Shocked, she tried to calm me down and said that I must not jump to conclusions without getting to the root of the matter; to wait till she got home before I did anything I may regret later. I did as I was asked, but the gleam had gone out of my heart and I was really incredibly depressed.

When as usual Keith returned home later that evening at his normal time, I told him about what had happened. Well, without batting an eyelid, he said coolly, 'I have not been feeling well for the past three days and therefore have not been going to work.' 'Then why didn't you tell me this earlier? You could have rested here at home,' I responded. He replied, 'I did not wish to worry you unnecessarily, so I used to leave at the regular time and rest in my own room and return here at my normal office time.' This explanation wholly convinced me and I made him promise that he would never again hide anything from me. He agreed and we made up; and by the time my parents returned, all was well again and the matter was dropped.

Just a week before 1 November, the date originally fixed for the wedding, Keith had to undergo a minor surgery for a torn ankle ligament. It was therefore on 6 of November 1982 that I signed the marriage register at a quiet ceremony in our own drawing room. After all the upheavals in my love life, I was finally married, and most importantly, to the man of my choice.

We were to have a proper church wedding once Keith's parents had reconciled themselves to our marriage, so the registered wedding was kept a low profile affair. However, as far as our family was concerned, Keith and I were man and wife, and were hereafter to live with my parents. Dressed in a beautiful wine-red and gold sari, I moved among the few guests present at the mini-wedding. Everyone congratulated me; happy and relieved, I for the first time felt a heavy load lift off my soul. Everyone present was rapturous about the development, and there was a lavish dinner to celebrate the event.

Presently, the guests departed and it was time to retire into our bedroom where I could now at last, lie in the caring and loving arms of my wonderful husband. So it was that, with a blend of happiness and nervousness, playing hide-and-seek in my heart, I walked into our bedroom to find Keith waiting for me, half sitting, half lying on the bed. And the moment I shut the door behind me, I froze at the sight of my wedding surprise. Never before had I heard or experienced anything such as the scene that presented itself. Keith began flinging appalling abuses and threats at my family and me, making comments that he would now show us all what he was actually made of... he was not going to be treated like a servant... that I only knew the good side of him and now he was going to let me have it nice and proper... he would ensure we all would pay dearly for all we have subjected him to. In all my twenty-two years, I had never before heard the kind of abusive language, which totally stunned and terrified me out of my wits.

I could not figure out what had suddenly hit me; everything had been completely enchanting and joyful till a couple of minutes ago; what had so suddenly triggered off such violence in this wonderful individual? Then, imagining something was really troubling him, I stepped forward trembling all over and began asking what was wrong. This made matters even worse, and he now began flinging his arms around violently as if to strike me, and threatened to awaken my parents and give them a piece of his mind too.

Terrified by this thought, and too shocked by the bewildering phenomenon, I heard him begin to vomit violently right there. That is when it struck me that he had probably had too much to drink, which too came as a shock to me, as he always swore to have nothing to do with hard liquor. I tried to help as best I could; wiping his face and getting him some cold water, but he simply flung me aside. I therefore had no alternative but to wait till he was exhausted and slumped on the bed and fell asleep.

The storm that had so suddenly struck from nowhere, halted just as abruptly, leaving in its wake, soiled bed-covers, a stinking, and filthy floor, and heaps of shattered dreams. I spent the remainder of my wedding night weeping and clearing up the disarray and wondering what I had got myself into.

Was this what I had been praying for all these years? Wasn't I better off without a husband? What had I done wrong to have deserved this? Why was God punishing me so? What hurt me the most was the suffering it would cause my parents and brother when they discovered what had happened. How was I going to hide this from them? I hoped no one had heard anything.

The following morning, my mother did ask me whether something was the matter, because the previous night she had heard funny noises emanating from our room. Feeling embarrassed and also not wanting to hurt her, I replied, 'No Ma, Keith was a little unwell, that's all,' and superficially all seemed to be fine; Keith had absolutely no recollection of the night's episode.

'Thank God,' I thought with relief, 'the hurt was only mine and mine alone.' All was not however as it used to be; the fiery, happy girl had died last night, leaving in her place a frightened, sad, and insecure young woman. Although he probably did not actually remember the episode of the wedding night, there was a marked indifference in his attitude towards me. He lay in bed till almost midday, then dressed, poured himself a gin and lime, and spent the rest of the day in front of the television. Again, at about seven in the evening, he poured himself some rum and coke, once more lay watching TV till it was time for dinner. Then, on the second night, when I entered the room, he asked me lovingly, 'What is the matter with you today? Why are you walking around with a long face? Do you wish to demonstrate to everyone that you are not happy with me?'

I made an attempt to smile, but before I could reply, he was hissing again, 'You will never be satisfied... no matter what I do to you.' Hurt and scared as I was after the previous night's experience, I began weeping; words failed me, and this brought me a volley of abuses. In the morning however, when I took him his cup of tea, he asked me to sit down, apologized for the previous night's behaviour, and promised that this would never happen again.

Ecstatic with relief, hope flooded into my entire being. I thought that at last, things are going to be fine! They actually were for a few days, till I requested him to refrain from drinking incessantly, as this was certain to ruin his health. The temporary calm was broken and he began shouting abuses and threatening to leave me. He marched around the house like a big bully. Unconcerned that he was being overheard by my mother, he asked me to mind my own business and not to try ruling his life. Frightened out of my wits, I found myself apologizing for what, I do not know. I begged him to be silent because I did not at any cost want to upset others in my home. He did then calm down, and I myself spoke as little as possible, lest I annoy him again.

With my wedding having changed the course of my life so drastically, my self-esteem and confidence crushed and diminished, I went about life as if in a nightmare! Everything went by in the haze of confused emotion. There was no news of the church wedding taking place; that too seemed to have become a forgotten event; nor was there any likelihood of any kind of reconciliation with my in-laws.

Subsequently, in December, Uncle Surjeet came to India from Germany for a vacation and was to be around until the second week of January, following which it was planned to finalize our church wedding on 3 January 1983.

It was like all usual weddings, with loads of shopping, invitations, and other such preparations. So on a shivery 3 January afternoon, clad in a simple white gown with a slender white sash, with a tiny blue flower and a long white veil pinned to the crown of my head with an delicate white wreath, and clutching a bouquet of flowers, I ascended the stairs of the beautiful St Thomas's Church on my father's arm. At the entrance, Keith awaited me, looking extremely handsome and virtuous in a dark blue suit with a red rose in the lapel of his jacket. (Seeing him there, who would have believed the cruel tyrant he had been to me in private.)

Daddy gave me away to him at the entrance and the two of us walked together to the front of the church, followed by Keith's cousin Lesley, the bridesmaid, and Sandy, the best man. The church was full of relatives and friends and as soon as we were settled in the front pews, the priest, dear Father Iris, began the wedding mass. Shivering with cold and fear, having nothing to look forward to, I sorrowfully took the marriage vows. The cold wedding band slid on to my finger; confirming my conviction of having to spend the rest of my life suffering atrocities and humiliation at my husband's hands, as we were once more, pronounced 'man and wife' in the presence of the Lord.

The ceremony was followed by a reception, and later, there was a small dinner party at our home for close family and friends. Strangely, once the wedding was over, and we were home, I remember waltzing happily away to some very beautiful country music in our drawing room, with a sense that all might now turn out to be just perfect. This was probably because I knew Keith was an ardent believer in his religion, and now that our marriage had been sanctified in church, he too would be a truly happy man.

Following the wedding, Keith resumed work and was out almost all day, while I too fell into the routine of everyday living. A few weeks later, I found I was expecting my first baby. This was excellent news, for I loved babies and now I was to have one of my very own. Keith too was very happy and wanted a daughter whom he would call Marian. Crossing my fingers, praying and relieved, I went about handling my new condition and preparing for the new member to arrive.

A few weeks later, I accompanied Keith to Chandigarh, where he was to be for a fortnight for a book fair. We were staying with my grandparents, and though Keith would be out all day, I very much looked forward to spending the evenings and mornings with him. This was however not to be: from the very first evening, he came home almost near midnight; steeped in alcohol, out of his senses, I was the recipient of the usual verbal and physical abuse. The fact that I was pregnant did not matter, that we were at my grandparents' was totally ignored; he simply tortured me every night without fail. Fed up and helpless, I attempted to end my life by swallowing half a bottle of rum, which I found, stored away in his office bag. Fortunately, it did not kill me and fortunately too, it did not wreak any damage to my unborn little one either. I was just very ill for a few days.

Then one evening, completely out of the blue, came the next blow: Keith came home with the news that he had given up his job. Deep concern must have been writ large on my face as he hastened to reassure me, 'Don't worry Penny, I will soon get another one. There are plenty of jobs in the market, but I wish to start my own business instead of working so hard for someone else.'

His thoughtful consideration and plans, for the future brought me momentary relief, till his next proposition sunk home. 'Ask your father to give me about Rs 10,000 to start my business, which I will return as soon as my work begins to bring in money,' he demanded. Feeling uneasy and rotten, I did as I was told. With the entire financial burden upon my father's salary, I knew very well how difficult it was for Daddy to cough up this extra money, but the sum was arranged and handed over to my husband with absolutely no questions asked.

Months passed, and Brown Book Distributors was still only a name on Keith's lips. No business began, no work was undertaken, no money came, and my stress soared sky high. My pregnancy was advancing; I was reeling under unknown and unexpected physical as well as emotional pressures; suffering in solitude and silence. There was no one with whom I could share my pain; sharing my troubles with my family would only aggravate the difficulties my situation was causing them. Nothing could bring me to do that; all I did was cry silently and search for solutions, and they too seemed to have deserted me at this time.

Life had totally let me down, I thought; I had stepped out to lessen the burden on my parents and brother; but all I had succeeded in achieving was to have aggravated it manifold. Earlier, it was only me they had to look after; but now it was my husband, and there was my baby coming who would be on their hands too.

What was I to do? I often tried to discuss the issue with Keith, but he either picked up a fight with me or painted a rosy picture and brushed off the matter. On top of that, he was never truthful and was once again shouting at me and abusing me almost all the time. He spent every day playing carom or going to movies with friends, while I laboured each day under the tension and guilt of being so helplessly and hopelessly dependent upon my loving family. My parents and Sandy did their best to comfort my aching heart, but I was unable to forgive myself for the anguish I had innocently brought into our home. I began to derive consolation in the thought of dying in childbirth.

Deep down, I was well aware that putting an end to my life would only bring unbearable pain to those who I loved so dearly; so the least I could do was to remain alive and hope for the best. I was well aware that I had already brought them far more than their share of trouble, and that just for my sake, they had lived with my blindness and the various hardships it brought with it, and that I therefore owed them my life at the very least. I therefore continued living, passing each day, trying to care for my unborn child, knitting little sweaters and caps, taking care of my health, going for walks, and helping my mother with the housework!

No matter how hard I tried to divert my attention from the unpleasantness of the present situation, I would often catch myself weeping quietly in some corner or the other. 'How could I continue to live a life of total dependency forever? How would my child feel when she discovered that her parents were good for nothing; even the woman who had brought her into this world was completely helpless and would eventually only remain a burden? Until when would we live as a source of bother and extort unjustifiable advantage from others?' There wasn't a moment when I was free of such thoughts; it was as if a bottomless pit of despair had descended upon me that was sucking me in from which I knew not how to extract myself.

Soon, it was time for me to appear for the class 10 examination. I wondered how I would manage as my concentration was focused on my life's dilemma alone, and I totally lacked the energy or will to prepare for the exam. Also, of course, Keith had given up reading to me as soon as he had proposed marriage, but I did somehow appear for the exam and passed.

By the time the baby was to be born, Keith had finished squandering away the money he had borrowed, leaving us penniless. He still went out every day, to heaven knows where, and on most evenings, returned half drunk and perfectly happy; and to avoid being questioned, he gave us the 'leave me alone' signal by shutting doors noisily or simply huffing about one or another. To evade any unpleasantness at home, I dared not utter a word or make a sign that may meet his wrath or displeasure, yet constantly feared his unpredictable outburst of abuse or sarcasm. I was even made fun of; Keith would hand me an empty plate after rattling an empty serving spoon on it, then urge me to eat, saying with sarcastic mirth, 'Here eat!' And when I put my hand on the plate searching for the food, he would have a hearty laugh!

It was absolutely extraordinary that a man who had been as caring and empathetic as the Keith I had known earlier could do this to me day after day. Till the time I married him, I had never felt I was blind, but now my blindness was rubbed into me as often as was possible: 'Hey you blind bat...,' he would yell, 'What do you think of yourself? You should thank your stars I married you... don't you all ever forget it,' would be his favourite monologue. These words stung my very being; I felt stifled and indignant. Deeper and deeper, I submerged into self-pity and the further my mind receded into the clutches of terror, forever expecting to be lashed out at. I lived for moments when Keith was away, intensely dreading his return. Being accustomed to an atmosphere of intense love and sensitivity, such insulting behaviour and callousness was proving much too difficult to cope with. My acutely sensitive persona was becoming more and more battered with each passing day, and was simply being reduced to tears and depression.

With the birth of my baby drawing closer, my coping mechanism was cracking, resulting in dangerous nervous spasms of my lower body. Remarkably, I was not at all fearful of the approaching childbirth; instead, I was almost looking forward to a possible escape, by dying in the process. Therefore, when the initial delivery pains set in the early hours of 23 September 1983, I felt oddly relieved and excited; the beginning of the end of all sufferings was upon me. Once again, I was lighthearted and energetic as I underwent the 20-hour ordeal.

I was most surprised at the very mild discomfort of the contractions I experienced, given the horrifying tales I had heard about the pains and pangs of childbirth. In fact, for most of the day there was no pain, just a strange sensation in my lower body, which hardly inhibited me from going about my daily business. As the day progressed, curiously, all negativity of the past months magically disappeared and was replaced with a glowing sense of expectancy.

Keith had just recovered from a bad bout of flu and was at home too, but, for a change, he too seemed happy. There were no unkind words or scolding today… all seemed, as it should be on a day such as this. Mummy kept a close vigil on my condition with a doctor next door visiting me, and at about 8 p.m., we prepared to go to the hospital as the sensations increased in frequency and intensity. Feeling fairly comfortable and confident, wondering where the much talked about agonizing pains had gone, I arrived at the Sector 6 Government Maternity Hospital. There was coolness in the air and a few drops of rain floated down as I alighted from my father's Fiat and walked into the dimly lit entrance hall of the hospital. After making a few inquiries, Mummy and I went up to the first floor, while Keith, Daddy, and Sandy waited in the hall downstairs.

Mummy was permitted to accompany me into the ward adjoining the labour room only because of my blindness. The place was ablaze with lights (up to then I was able to see the light and if I stuck my nose close enough, I could also see some forms). It was about 10.30 at night and the room was milling with groaning and moaning women, hustling and bustling nurses, and formidable sounding doctors. I was led to a stretcher on one side of the ward and asked to lie down. A young lady doctor did a matter-of-fact examination of my tummy, muttered a few instructions to the nurse, and left. The nurse asked me to get off the stretcher and requested my mother to wait outside while she led to and sat me down on a bed close by, which was already occupied by two other groaning women. Before I could park myself on the edge of this bed, one of the suffering woman turned her crying face to me and said, 'Please help me sister, I am in terrible pain and they have given me this gown to wear and I am not able to get into it. Saying this, she half gave and half flung the green hospital gown at me, accompanied by shrieks of tormenting pain. Taking the gown away from my face, I helped the poor soul with it, while answering her inquiry about my identity, 'I too am here to deliver my baby,' I said with a smile. 'It doesn't seem so sister,' she gasped, as the next bout of contractions must have taken hold.

Assuring her of my intentions, I stepped away from the bed as the other lady decided to roll on to the side where I was about to sit. Before I could congratulate myself upon my narrow escape from the danger of landing on the floor, my gown was being violently pulled from behind by another lady in severe distress. With great alacrity, I saved myself from losing my balance by clutching on to a passing nurse.

The commotion had made me forget my own purpose of being there and unable to suppress my giggling, I hung on to the arm of this kind nurse, who immediately led me away to safety of a vacant bed on the far side of the room.

'We are going to give all of you an injection to induce sleep and reduce the pain,' announced one of the nurses with a syringe between her fingers. 'Well, Sister,' I answered, 'I think I am here to have my baby, and would rather do that than sleep.' 'The doctor is not going to undertake any further deliveries tonight,' explained the kind nurse who had rescued me, 'so we have been instructed to put everyone off to sleep with a mild sedative.' 'If you don't mind, I do not desire it and anyway, I am not experiencing any pain at all at the moment,' I said, determined to get on with whatever it was that was to happen. 'Your case seems perfectly normal Preeti,' declared Sister Jyotsna, (a fairly senior nurse) 'if you so wish and put your trust in me, I will handle your case myself,' she offered kindly. 'I have been delivering babies for the last 30 years and if you do as I say,' she smiled, 'you will have your baby in your arms much before the night is over.' I readily accepted the offer and she was as good as her word… in less than two hours, and with only three very painful final contractions, I was mother to the most beautiful baby girl in the world.

It was a moment of pure bliss when I heard my little baby cry her first little cries. 'Had I been able to create a human life?' As all mothers will agree, no music is anywhere as enchanting as their baby's first cries. I had always wanted a daughter, and God had bestowed me with a little doll. Keith too was in raptures at the birth of his daughter, and this gave me hope that this would generate a rapport that would bind us together once more. I longed to see my little girl through the eyes of the man whom I still seemed to love so much.

Nothing of the sort of course happened. My longing and waiting for just a few soothing words, proved in vain. It was the baby that took up all his attention and I was kind of left out completely. I was just fortunate enough to be allowed to choose 'Fiona' as my baby's name, and before long, the novelty of the new baby wore off, and the shouting and abuse was resumed for no particular reason. 'This is how I am,' he once told my mother, 'and she had better learn to live with it.'

My health began to reflect my state of mind. Although the recipient of loving care showered upon me by my family, post-delivery recovery was hardly visible. Besides, in addition, by the time little Fiona was 12 weeks old; I had to go in for an abortion. Due to acute weakness and shortage of blood, I could not have gone through with a second pregnancy. Following this, I suffered from serious back pain and was on bed rest for six weeks. Then, even before I had time to recover, 6 months later I was pregnant again. Our second baby had made up its mind to come anyway.

By this time, with God's grace, a friend of Keith's had helped him to secure a job as assistant manager in a reputed publishing house. Once again, I had found a reason to be happy; I was now the wife of an assistant manager and a proud mother of a beautiful daughter. If things kept progressing in this way, I thought, life would gradually settle down. It would have been tough enough for me to bring up two children on my own, but given my blindness, I was really happy to have the loving support of my parents and brother.

Keith was apparently happy with his new job and would hopefully allow us to live in peace. Gradually, during my second pregnancy, my health improved considerably. Following the harrowing experience of my first confinement, Holy Family hospital was selected for my second baby's birth.

It was 4 February 1985; I was preparing to go for my routine check-up, when I felt something trickling down between my legs. 'I wonder what that could be,' I thought to myself and continued to drape my sari. My tummy felt funny too, and I kept experiencing an insistent urge to go to the washroom, yet when I did, nothing came out... 'Appears as if something has upset my stomach,' I told myself; when the next few drops of the warm liquid dribbled down my thighs.

Alarmed and anxious at this strange occurrence, I tried to discover what it was. It smelt like blood, I thought, but I was not completely convinced as I could not of course see it. But I was pregnant, so how could that possibly be? Who do I ask? There was no one in the house, and it would be absurd to ask my neighbours to inspect my underwear. An hour later, Ma came home and she confirmed my doubts: it was indeed blood. I was immediately rushed to the hospital and was placed under intensive care. And on this occasion, I was really facing the threat of bleeding to death; and unfortunately, now I had every reason and the desire to live. I had little Fiona and now there was my second baby, so on no account was I going to allow life to cheat on me. The doctors believed whatever they wished, but I was confident that both the baby and I would emerge from the hospital in perfect health.

By the evening, my family returned home, leaving me in hospital, for an indefinite period. Remarkably, rather than feeling frightened and lost, for the first time in years I slept like a log. Although aware of my critical condition, as I lay in the clean comfort of the hospital bed, I was in high spirits with a calm heart; I reunited with my long lost friends, 'peace and freedom'.

Here, there was no one to shout and abuse me; the tyrant having limited access to the hospital's female ward. I was extremely happy, because, besides being out of Keith's clutches, I was being spoilt and comforted by the wonderful nurses. In addition, here, Keith acted the perfect doting husband and dutifully visited me as often as possible, lest his reputation suffer.

Usually, I passed the time contentedly, chatting with fellow patients, eating and sleeping, and generally observing the world go by. Even though the bleeding had more or less subsided, I had been prescribed complete bed rest in hospital till the baby's birth, which meant at least 10 weeks. You see, my placenta had come down, and was perpetually attempting to push its way out prematurely, posing a serious threat to both the baby's and my own life. In any event, the doctors referred to me as a 'time bomb', as I might hemorrhage at any moment, which would give me only a 50 per cent prospect of survival.

All this notwithstanding, I was the happiest patient around because no degree of physical pain and discomfort, even if laced with the threat of death, could dampen the relief of being away from the suffering imposed by Keith's company. Anxiety for my baby's life or my own never concerned me; oddly, I was quite certain we would both be fine, no matter what others thought. Many people asked me wonderingly, 'Aren't you scared Preeti, knowing that, anything can happen to your baby or you?' To this, I would reply laughingly, 'Nothing is going to happen to us; we are both on holiday here!' My inner feelings proved accurate, as on the twentieth day of my hospitalization, little Mark arrived via an emergency operation. Hurray, we were both still alive. Little Mark was really 'little', weighing 1.45 kg, and then over the next few days, dropped to an alarming low of 900 gm. The poor little mite had ventured out of the fortification of his mother's womb at 28 weeks and 3 days of pregnancy, and now had to fend for himself, tucked away in an oxygen bag with needles supplying him with food and blood. I was discharged from the hospital, while the little sweetheart spent the next three months in the hospital nursery under the loving care of the nurses and doctors.

On the day following my discharge, I contracted high fever and was re-admitted for treatment. Although, I stayed in hospital for over a month, I was not permitted to visit little Mark for fear that I would transmit my infection to him. However, my unwelcome fever gave me the advantage of being provided with a 'round the clock' update on the condition of my newborn, and I am certain he too felt that 'mummy' was close at hand.

About five weeks later, I was sent home again, to once more await the return of my baby. Although it felt good to be home with my family and little Fiona, my short-lived peace once again vanished. Panic attacks plagued me at the thought of now losing my beautiful children, and haunted me day and night. 'How could someone like me, doomed with such ill luck, have been granted the good fortune of having two beautiful normal children?' I would think. 'Could I deserve such good fortune; surely something really bad was about to befall. What would that be? This must surely be just a lull before a storm.' Hallucinations of us perishing in a natural disaster or a nuclear war tormented me day and night. I was so scared, I could neither eat, nor sleep; everyone and everything was hidden from my awareness under a veil of horror, expecting greater suffering to descend upon me at any moment. You can imagine my plight; I was both mentally and physically weak and vulnerable, abused and taunted by my husband, and in addition, completely helpless, dependant, and disabled. 'How would I look after my two children? Where would the money come from? How much a greater burden had I become staying on with my parents? However, given the husband I had, what was the alternative?' were the thoughts that constantly passed through my mind and nagged me.

Then finally one day, when I could bear it no longer, I picked up the courage to share my distress with my mother. She smiled encouragingly and said, 'Do you think you are the only one in the world who has two normal children? Stop being silly; everyone has children and nothing is going to happen to yours. No one has the time to harm your little ones, so forget about it and get on with taking care of them.' Her words had the required effect, and besides having the little ones to look after helped me to regain the balance I had lost.

To our delight, little Mark returned from hospital after three long months. With a head as large as a hen's egg and eyes as big as green cardamoms, Mummy would bathe him in a saucepan placed on the dining table lest he drown in anything larger. She was instructed to feed him every one and a half hours round the clock; so eventually she was the 'mom' as my blindness ruled me out of handling such a fragile little baby.

Thus, blessed with two darling children, and also burdened with a snarling husband, the journey of life jolted along. Then, as the years passed I noticed my fear and humiliation suddenly transforming into anger.

There are so many incidents that come falling out of the closet of memory relating to this part of my life, but I choose to share just a few that tore me apart and left permanent scars on our lives.

Thankfully, Keith continued to hold on to his job, but the major chunk of his salary went towards his own entertainment. If he was ever in a good mood or felt he had to make up with me, we were given gifts of varying value, and taken for outings. Whether it was entertaining friends or purchasing the bare necessities of everyday life, or funding education, my parents were unquestioningly held responsible. Keith had established himself as the ruler of my parents' home and never hesitated to express his displeasure if his wishes were in any way ignored. He came and went as he pleased, did exactly what he wished, regardless of how it might affect any of us. Just to maintain peace at home, none of us dared raise objections to anything he said or did.

The less any of us protested, the greater the advantage he took of this. He was out almost every evening, would throw tantrums if the food was not to his taste, snatched pieces of chocolate out of children's mouths and ate it himself while the children cried at being cheated. If at all the kids dared to disobey him, they were mercilessly struck with whatever he could lay his hands on. Abusing and poking fun at the three of us was his favourite pastime. He spent a large part of his time running errands for friends and neighbours, lending a shoulder to sad and lonely women, solving their problems, while his own wife and children craved for just a few moments of love and care. He slept through nights when the children were seriously ill and the rest of the family rushed around tending to them. If he felt in the mood, he would play with them, if not, he physically beat them and chased them away. 'Why don't you run away fast when papa hits you, silly; don't you see I fly off when I see his hand coming,' Fiona would say to little Mark, who would cling on to his father even after being slapped hard. If I on my part tried to defend the poor little things, I would be screamed at and their punishments would be harsher. 'You,' he would address me, 'you better lay off! These are my children and I can do as I please with them. I will see how you stop me from hitting them… I am going to send them away to boarding school as soon as they are five,' he threatened. Terrified, I would begin weeping, while he got back to screaming and shunting the innocent dears around.

Then, there were the numerous instances of utter embarrassment and humiliation, when Keith headed straight for the liquor cabinet, and drank till he collapsed. Can you for a moment imagine my plight? I couldn't see, and Keith would be too drunk to drive us home. We have, on many occasions, survived fatal accidents just by sheer good luck. There seemed to be no solution to this, for refusing to accompany him to places which I had been invited would mean asking for trouble, and accompanying him meant disgrace and risk. If I remained silent at a party, he was displeased; if, on the other hand, I socialized, I was accused of flirtation. According to him, I did nothing right; I was crazy and stupid, he told his friends.

I did everything in my power to keep the children from going out with us, lest they become innocent victims of their father's drunken driving. I myself have however been flung out on to the road in front of a speeding bus; have been thrown into a four feet deep drain, have been dragged up the stairs accompanied by vile abuses, to cite just a few instances. In addition, I have been witness to his passing out at many a party, and having to spend the night at the mercy of strangers. Nothing could prevent him to keep a control on from engaging in his indiscreet alcohol consumption; least of all, the care of his wife and children.

What good was he as a husband and father? He did not love or care for us; he hardly ever provided for any of our needs either. He was never with us, in happiness or in sorrow; only making life hell for everyone. If he ever did do anything good for any of us, it would only be to win the appreciation of outsiders. You will indeed be surprised to learn how entirely successful he was in this.

People beyond our four walls swore by his goodness. 'There is no one as wonderful and caring as Keith,' they would echo, 'you can depend upon him with your life.' What a wonderful act of kindness to have married a blind girl. 'He severed relations with his own parents just in order to look after her entire family. He works, cooks, and cleans; tends to the children and beyond this, attends to their school work too. How fortunate of her to have found a blessing like dear Keith. And beyond all this, he is in church every week without fail,' This was the general impression that prevailed, except amongst the very few who saw through his charade.

On a fateful day in 1986, Keith got home from work a little earlier than his usual time and found both Mummy and me away shopping. When we returned, seeing the pack of sanitary napkins in my hand, (which had been paid for by Mummy), he scornfully said, 'You shameless woman, look at the way you go around squandering money. Do you have any idea of how hard it is to earn ten rupees?' and before I could recover from the stinging taunt, he went on, 'Here I slog my backside off to make ends meet; and all you do is blow it all up. On top of that, you and your mother don't have the decency to be here to receive me when I return home from a hard day's work!' This time he had struck too hard. My aching mind and soul were completely shattered; I would die if I was to continue to live like this for any longer. Something burst inside me; turning around I marched out of the room. For the first time since I had married this man, tears failed to emerge. Anger flared within, bringing to life my dormant self respect, and I simply vowed that I will earn Rs 10,000 and show him how money is earned! Keith had done his job; I was wide-awake and alive again.

The mistake I was making suddenly became crystal clear to me. Whatever was going wrong, I realized with shock that it was I who had to change, and the key to this lay within me. I understood with utter precision that crying around, waiting for him to change into my prince charming would never be the answer. I had to do something completely different, to bring about positive change into our lives. It was as if a switch in my mind had been turned on... it began to think again.

Problems seemed to have been pushed aside; solutions were being sought. Days passed, weeks went by without any workable idea presenting themselves. All kinds of plans popped in and out of my mind... I would take up a job... but before I could even begin to work upon it, counter thoughts and fear shot them down. Who will give me a job with just a class ten certificate? I could begin to take music classes... but I was out of touch and knew too little about music any how, and it would take too long to brush up my own skills. I could take on some typing work, but from where? And it was too poorly paid for the kind of time and effort it entailed, and then who would check my errors?

I thought of opening a day care facility for children of working mothers, but it was difficult enough to look after the two of my own, so how could I care for others? So it went on and on; months passed without a workable solution germinating. On the other hand, matters were worsening by the day between the two of us as my pain had by then been transformed into a raging frustration. Every time I felt hurt or upset, I would retaliate through open verbal battles, subjecting the children to unpleasantness and suffering. Though I did feel sorry for the poor dears, I could not help being irritable and impatient almost all the time. It was very strange that from the quiet and peace-loving individual I had been, I was becoming an aggressive retaliator. I agreed that it had been my mistake to have married this man, and that I hadn't been able to handle my post-marriage situation in the way I should have. However, mistakes can and must be rectified and forgiven; for nothing must be allowed to wreck lives forever; all of us deserved a dignified and contented life.

To achieve such a life, I had to first become a contributor. I felt that Keith should not be held totally responsible for the disharmony in our relationship; as an equal partner, I too was accountable. The foundation of a happy family was built on the basis of mutual love and understanding, respect, trust, and forgiveness. Money too was a major element to happy family life. As I possessed all of the above in abundance apart from money, I decided to look for ways of making it.

I was well aware that emotionally I loved Keith and the children very much, and to see us happy, I was prepared to do anything. I therefore truly believed that once I could help supplement the family income, the missing pieces would fall in place and abundant happiness would be ours. I was just twenty-six and we had our whole life ahead; it never is too late to begin.

Almost after a year of such self-motivation, along with various profession-hunting contemplations, in September 1987 the idea of running aerobic classes struck me. I was motivated by Veena Merchant's 'Keep Fit Show'. I thought that if people could exercise along with the television, I was certain they would love to workout with a real life person. It wouldn't matter if their teacher was blind, so long as I was able to provide them with a workout worth their money. Working out with me would certainly be better than with a TV screen.

Nothing negative about this scheme tempered my boundless enthusiasm. I lost no time in locating the phone number of the Delhi Television office and after five or six attempts, managed to acquire Ms Veena Merchant's phone number, and hours later, I was actually speaking to her.

'May I speak to Ms Merchant,' I enquired over the phone, my voice quivering with nervous excitement! My heart missed a beat when I heard the voice reply, 'This is Veena,' in a kindly tone, 'what can I do for you?' Without a moment's delay, I blurted, 'I am Preeti, a blind person, and I would like to join your instructor training programme.' I held on tightly to the receiver, awaiting her reply, 'Well, Preeti,' she said, 'you are welcome to join my classes and workout with us, but I am afraid I don't think the instructor training programme is the right thing for you.' A little impatient but not discouraged, I went on, 'Could I please come and meet you madam.' 'Yes, of course,' she replied, 'I live in Safdarjung Enclave and you can come tomorrow morning any time after 9.30 a.m.' Thrilled to bits, I quickly thanked her, took her address and hung up. Sharp at 9.30 a.m. the following morning, heart thumping with incalculable anticipation, I stepped off Keith's scooter outside Veena Merchant's gate. Stepping into her office, nervous but eager, I awaited the opportunity of convincing her of my ability to take up the profession of an aerobic instructor despite my blindness.

Presently, a short energetic figure entered the office from a door behind me. Standing up, I turned to introduce myself when my hand was warmly clasped by a small yet firm one; 'Hello, my dear,' she said in a strong deep feminine voice, 'I guess you are Preeti?' Not waiting for my reply, she went on, 'I am Veena. Why don't you sit down and tell me what I can do for you?' She went around the table, greeted Keith with a handshake, and turned to me. Once again, I repeated my request, 'I have come here to be allowed to join the instructor training programme; how do I go about doing so?'

Hesitating for a moment, she replied, 'How am I going to teach you to become an instructor, my dear? I have been checking with people in the US for information or guidelines regarding this, but from what I have learnt from my research is that up to now, nowhere in the world has there been a blind aerobic instructor,' she said with great sympathy.

'Please madam,' I persisted politely, not taking the evident negative response for an answer, 'do please consider giving me at least one opportunity to join the class and I am sure I will manage.' 'But how am I to teach you?' she protested, 'I have never ever up to this day even known a blind person, so how will I be able to teach you,' she said sadly. Sensing the apparent discomfort in the room, Keith got up and took himself off; anyhow, surprisingly, he had not uttered a word till then. Veena too rose from her chair and made a move to dismiss me politely, 'I will give you this form; please fill it in and you will be most welcome to come and work out with us from tomorrow,' she was saying. 'Madam,' I said, disregarding her words, 'all you will need to do is to allow me into the instructor training class, agree to answer a few of my questions when the class is on, and leave the rest to me,' I pleaded, showing no signs of leaving her office.

'Alright then Preeti,' sighed Veena, 'then please get yourself track pants along with a pair of joggers, and I will see you here at 7.00 tomorrow morning.' Jumping out of the chair where I had sat so adamantly, I leaned across the table between us, hugged Veena, and thanked her profusely. I left feeling the bitter sweetness of my first success.

On the way home, I requested Keith to take me directly to the Sarojini Nagar market, from where I bought a pair of relatively expensive, locally made joggers, and decided to borrow his track pants.

Keith was strangely silent throughout this eventful morning; he had never so much as mildly protested at my spending Rs 300 on my joggers, and in any event, I was too thrilled to dwell on this for more than a few seconds; I was alight with ecstasy!

The sun had dawned on the horizon of life... with a real promise of a fantastic future ahead. I was prepared to work as hard as was required and would surpass my best; after all, this appeared to be the missing link to the life of my dreams. So, with a pledge to make amends to all those who had been injured by my mistakes, I stepped into a startled Veena's instructor training class.

I say 'startled Veena' as that is exactly what she was; she told me later that she had only agreed to my admission simply to get rid of me. Well, now that I was there, Veena put me with the others facing the instructor, while she took up her position beside me. The music commenced, and so did the instructions. It didn't seem difficult to begin with. Charlie, the instructor, was teaching both via visual and verbal instructions and anything I was not able to follow were shown to me by Veena physically, pulling and pushing my arms and legs. The very next thing that I remember was, lying on my back on the matted floor, water splashing over my face and people crowding around me. 'Are you OK Preeti,' the jumble of voices came rushing at me. 'You are too weak Preeti,' said Veena in her strong soft way, 'this is not for you; you fainted within five minutes of starting the workout; and now I think you had better go home.' I immediately pushed aside the fussing crowd, jumped on to my feet and responded, 'Oh no madam,' I assured my teacher, 'I am perfectly fine and will remain right here. Apologies for the fainting, shall we carry on now?'

Thereafter, under Veena's guidance, I underwent a disciplined fitness-building regime, complete with controlled nutrition and a six-hour per day exercise programme. Within three months of that day in September, I was teaching Veena's classes and in April 1988, I had launched my own aerobic regime.

Within three months of the launch of 'Preeti's Keep Fit' classes, I had transformed into a confident self-assured woman. Luck seemed to have suddenly decided to shine on me, as students flocked to my aerobic classes from all over Delhi, bringing with them loads of money and fame. I never kept account of the money that was flowing in, simply placing the fistfuls of notes in a diary in the dresser.

Oddly, rather than having the desired positive effect, my new found financial contribution as well as professional success only triggered further negativity into my relationship with Keith. This became evident in Keith's unwarranted harsh protests and displeasure at having to undertake the simple task of driving me to my classes. Therefore, to avoid listening to his loud curses and grumbles early in the morning, Sandy took on the task of driving me to the class.

This arrangement too did not please Keith; he complained bitterly that 'you simply look for excuses to cut me off and team up with others so that you can have a good time on your own'. It was becoming evident that no matter what I did, he could not to be pleased. Keith's behaviour deteriorated and he would do anything in his power to hurt and distress the children and me. My efforts to improve matters had backfired all over again!

This time however, I was not going to crumble and give up; I had to surge ahead holding on to whatever little hope I had... I was sure things would work out for the best one day. I clenched my fists, ignored the pain that gnawed into my heart, and held on for dear life to all the encouragement and happiness my new-found profession churned up.

In June 1988, following my father's retirement, Mummy and Daddy were to go for a holiday to Ireland and Germany to visit my uncles. I was somewhat apprehensive about their being away for three months as the entire responsibility of running the home, my classes, as well as the children would devolve on me, not to mention, coping with my difficult and nasty husband. There was however, Sandy, to help out and I felt certain we would manage.

As fate would have it, however, the day following their departure, Sandy fell seriously ill, and my coping abilities were put to a real test. With my hands and head overflowing with work, worry, and emotional harassment, I was forced to depend upon Keith to get the kids ready for school at least before he disappeared for the day. That of course increased their risk of having to endure their father's wrath. They became terrified and suffered tremendous emotional pain because he would hit and abuse them freely, and hit them harder if they dared to cry.

Besides, unable to independently cope with responsibilities outside the home due to my disability, and the necessity of doing this for sheer survival, I was forced to seek help from beyond my familial circle. Circumstances compelled me to pick up the courage and humility to seek and accept all the assistance I could muster from friends and neighbours, acquaintances, and passersby. This period was to be one of the toughest trials of my life, but also proved an incredible learning and bonding opportunity for me. It was during this time that I met innumerable sincere and good people whom probably God had sent to assist me.

Among those were my aerobic class students and friends. Shami and Dolly would ever so often take me to and from the morning class, and, Vivek, Sandy's friend and colleague, fetched the children back from school almost every day. In addition, there was Sunil, a friend of Keith's, who was always there at my beck and call at any time of the day or night. These friends, not only gave me a hand in times of need, but also provided me with much-needed emotional strength. Their warm and caring support helped me to remain sane through this rough journey filled with concerns and demands of a five and three-year old, an afflicted brother, teaching two aerobic classes a day, a little dog and running the house in entirety, not to mention a nasty and alcoholic husband. I had never feared work, could do with minimal sleep and rest, but I reeled under the merciless emotional torture that Keith dealt out to the children and me. Seeing afflictions, Sunil always had a kind word or gesture to comfort me, which my parched spirit lapped up and converted into unfaltering power to endure the rough times with a smile.

To my relief, a few weeks later, Sandy completely recovered and I was happy once more. The worst seemed to be over now, and during this trying time, I had sadly realized that I needed to get rid of Keith for good. This resolution somehow, brought me a deep sense of peace, and from that day onwards, I stopped trying to win his love and approval. Subsequently, my inner voice told me that I had arrived at the correct solution to the most painful problem of my life. It was the most wonderful feeling that once I could have Keith out of our lives, we could all live free of dread. It was I who had brought on this adversity upon my family and the onus of extricating ourselves from his clutches too lay with me. Though I was aware of the tremendous strength and courage entailed in actually taking this huge step, I realized it was the only alternative.

At this juncture, I had come in contact with other blind persons; and had been greatly inspired by their talents and achievements. A whole new world of possibilities opened its arms and now the onus was on me to take the appropriate action and reach out to fulfill my dreams.

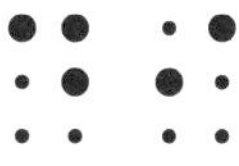

My meeting with Vimal Mohit, director of education at the National Association for the Blind (NAB) was another godsend opportunity to push me closer to realizing my dreams. Sunil had wanted to participate in a 'car rally for the blind' organized by the NAB, Delhi, and had taken me with him to the NAB where I later met this charismatic individual. Vimal later requested me to volunteer to teach aerobics to the blind children there. Naturally, I readily agreed, and from the next morning onwards, I began teaching aerobics to over a hundred blind students at the school. The children loved jumping and dancing to the beat of a drum and the instruction of my voice, while the teachers helped them to get the movements right. These classes infused a new and vibrant energy into me and added meaning and purpose to my existence. Gradually, I was drawn into the other activities at the institution, and was soon teaching English to the students and also counselling parents as well as learning other administrative responsibilities under Vimal's expert instruction.

My emotions could never be shared by two men at a time, and at the time, I still had Keith himself on my mind. His words and actions still continued to hurt and upset me. With such false allegations however, he succeeded in erasing forever the leftover sentiment in my heart of unconditional love for him. Though this had taken him six long years, he had finally, inadvertently, freed himself of my stubborn devotion, and in its place was left bleeding and hurtful wounds, petrifying fear, and yet a firm will to do the best I could for my little ones and myself!

All I now wanted was, to get rid of him as soon this could be managed. I eagerly awaited the return of my parents so that I could further muster up the courage to ask him to leave. The first week of October saw my parents at home, and I lost no time in telling them of my decision. Fortunately for me, they left the decision to me; but before I could do what was required, Sandy and I met with a scooter accident on our way to my morning aerobic class and were confined to bed rest for over two weeks. Although, neither of us had suffered serious injuries, my back hurt a lot, but my major concern at the time was the effect my condition might have upon my plan to separate from Keith.

'Don't you worry, Ma,' I cried, trembling in her arms as she opened the door to us when we returned from the site of the accident. 'I will very soon be fine... I don't seem to have been hurt too much. I will go back to taking classes... please don't stop me from sending Keith away.' She hugged me reassuringly and gently helped me lie down as I went on muttering, 'If by any chance, I cannot teach aerobics any longer because of my injury, I will take up the work of a housemaid... but nothing will ever induce me to any longer live in terror of Keith.'

I was back in class after three weeks; and thus the show was to continue. Although each day, I constantly thought of letting Keith know of my decision regarding the future of our relationship, the actual execution was proving far more difficult and scary than I had thought. Keith, for his part, was entirely oblivious of my intentions, was busy with his ruthless mistreatment of all the habitants of the house. That went on until one morning when he pushed his luck too far.

I had returned from the morning aerobic class along with two of my students, who were joining me for breakfast on that particular morning. Sitting with my two young friends in the drawing room, I went in to the washroom, where I was greeted with, 'Is this any time to come home? I find that you are flying too high for my liking... looks as if I will have to put a stop to all this.' Before I could hush him down, he went on with his voice rising higher, 'You think you are becoming too smart... you bloody blind bat.'

Not knowing where the idea or the courage came from, I simply pulled out a bag from under the mattress, thrust it towards Keith, and speaking with complete composure, I said, 'I really have had enough of your nonsense Keith and it is now about time you get the hell out of this house.' As the words left my lips, I automatically braced myself for violent retaliation but, none came. Instead, he began to packing up clothes from the open cupboard into the bag I had flung at him.

Leaving him in the act, I returned to the drawing room to join my friends, wondering what was to follow. A short while later, I heard Keith quietly leave the house as usual for his office, and the rustle of the plastic bag indicated that he had taken at least a few of his things.

At last I was able to thank heaven that the source of all our misfortunes was gone, hopefully never again to return to our lives. He certainly did not return that night, nor did we hear from him; and not for many more nights was there any news of him!

The long lost peace had returned to our home. The children might have missed him, but said very little to that effect. My sweet, sensitive, and caring mother felt very sorry for him, while my sense of fear and stress vanished, my spirit calmed.

After about three weeks, Keith telephoned my mother and begged her pardon; pleaded and cried to be given 'one chance' to make amends. He had realized his mistake; he lamented. He was miserable to be away from his beloved wife and children; that she should convey his plea to me and he assured her that he was now a changed man and would do all in his power to make the family happy if only she could convince me to take him back.

'It is very easy to break relationships, Penny my dear,' counselled my dear mother. 'He really seems to have understood the value of his family and whatever may have transpired. If there is of the slightest prospect of having the children grow up with both their parents, there is no harm in giving him one opportunity, but, this time we will ask him to take you and the children to his own home. Living with all of us may have been bothering him, and once it is his own set-up, I am sure things will resolve themselves,' she said.

The idea of my very own home appealed to me too, and I myself was not looking forward to a lonely life forever. Besides, I did not wish my children to be deprived of their father's love, and so I readily agreed to give it another chance.

Keith came back home and seemed a genuinely changed individual. The following months were very blissful as we went house-hunting and rented a lovely small two-room apartment in East Delhi, in close proximity to my parent's home. Early in 1989, we moved into our new home, with my parents and brother living nearby.

There was lots to do: the children had to be sent to school, the household chores done, and aerobic classes to be established in the new locality. However, as the months passed, and we were virtually settled in our everyday life, the mean streak in Keith began to resurface; and he was soon back to square one.

The children were mercilessly beaten for being children, and, just as earlier, any intervention on my part meant aggravating the situation manifold. Keith had once again lost his job and was forever drinking and being dishonest; the responsibilities of the home and kids were completely ignored. The children's bus fee, handed over to Keith by my father to pass on to the bus driver would never reach the driver; and we only discovered this when the driver himself asked my father to pay it.

All the promises made to my mother by the 'suffering' Keith were being broken a thousand times over. The ray of hope that had so eagerly been seized upon by me had long died out and in its place burnt flames of humiliation and hopelessness. How much longer would I be able to bear, Keith's cruelty and heartlessness? How was I to trust a compulsive liar who threatened and abused virtually all the time? With a sinking heart, I tried to pull along as best I could till one day, I almost flung myself off the second floor balcony to put an end to my life. I probably wasn't meant to die I guess, and therefore, Keith in his drunken state somehow caught hold of me and the fall was broken.

The children too must have felt unhappy and insecure in our house and thus found any number of little excuses to run off to their grandparents' home. Finally, when it became unbearable as well as unsafe to live with Keith, I confessed the ordeal I had been undergoing to my family. Disappointed and deeply saddened, they immediately took the kids and me back to the safety of their home.

Walking out of a home, one has to abandon a dream which no words can adequately express. Removing our belongings with trembling hands and packing them into suitcases. Then dragging the heavy bags down to the waiting car that had once brought them here, with a sense of celebration and bidding a final farewell to the kitchen that I had loved so well and to all the other belongings that must be left behind.

It was not only the four walls crammed with household goods from which I was parting, but I was being forced away from my own independent 'queendom'. Had Keith just lived up to even a fraction of his words, I would have somehow carried on.

Dry-eyed and besieged by such thoughts, I resettled our clothes, books, and other minor belongings I brought back to our new bedroom at my parents' sixth floor rented apartment in the society near the flat they were building for themselves. Although it was the same home I had left only a few months ago, it felt strangely unfamiliar, but safe. Oddly, neither Fiona nor Mark ever asked any questions about this abrupt change, just living life as it came I expect they realized for themselves why we were here. And why 'Keith Papa' had to be left behind.

The vast sums of money I had been earning had fallen to a trickle because the classes I had established in Madhuban had not gathered the same momentum as those in South Delhi. From these classes however, and also my voluntary work, there had sprung an opportunity for a short-term flow of income from the Ashoka Innovators of the Public, an international non-governmental organization which supports social entrepreneurs and change-makers with short-term projects. I had won a fellowship to teach aerobics to blind children to enhance their overall growth and responses to stimuli. I was now going to the NAB only thrice a week as the distance had substantially increased since our move to the trans-Yamuna area. In the meantime, Vimal from the NAB accompanied by his wife Anuradha had gone to the US for further studies, and he had died there following a heart attack. Most of my time now revolved around the children and my aerobic classes. I could no longer read with my magnifying glasses because, following my pregnancies, my residual vision had fallen to merely light perception. I had to therefore once again learn to do everything by touch, sound, smell, and guesswork.

Well, that's what life is all about. So before proceeding to sketch the rest of my memories for you, I would like to fill in a few small yet vital colours into the gaps that have been left in some interstices of this account. Alongside all that had been going on in my life, Sandy had been away in Bombay for about a year and a half. Little Chicki had lived her twelve long years and had left for her heavenly abode. Fiona now went to Mater Dei School and Mark to Don Bosco. Little Fiona was growing up, strong and lovely, and Mark too was becoming a big boy but was constantly plagued by severe seasonal asthma, which took a heavy toll on his education. Also of course, the conflict at home had very serious impact on their fragile little minds. The solitary silver lining that kept them on a relatively even keel was the loving care of their grandparents and uncle. They were growing up with the emotional burden of an unstable father and a helpless blind mother, while I suffered an immeasurable sense of guilt. Restlessness, arising from the emptiness of my life, clouded my thinking and I simply passed the days as they came with no goal other than a longing for peace. No thoughts came, no plans germinated, and knitting was all I occupied myself with when not struggling with the children.

Then, history began to repeat itself all over again. Keith began visiting the children in their schools and sending messages to us, pleading that we should return to him. He pleaded and cried to the innocent little souls that they should beg me on his behalf to forgive him just this once, lamenting that he couldn't bear to live without us. The children would come home from school with hope twinkling in their faces, 'Ma, you know Papa came today again… he is very sorry and says everything will now be OK forever.' 'Please Ma, give him just one more chance,' they would innocently plead, as if their world depended upon my consent. They never ever bothered me with any demands, never complained about anything; it broke my heart to see them suffer so. This devastated me and I experienced excruciating pain and immeasurable pity for the sweethearts; none of this was their fault, and I had no right to keep them away from paternal love! Alongside this, ever so often, Keith waited for my mother on the roadside outside our society building when she went shopping for vegetables, to beg her forgiveness and plead for that one last chance. This time, purely for the children's sake, I dug up the courage to return to Keith.

Just as before, we were welcomed with tears of love and joy by the man who never even batted an eye before subjecting us to incredible suffering. He had rejoined his old office and had found a new flat to rent in a new society. I couldn't help being happy too: new home, happy children, and a doting husband. It was altogether fantastic… God had eventually answered my prayers… the worst was finally over.

Life quickly fell into place, with children going to school, followed by homework and their playtime. While Keith and I shared the household chores, Sundays were spent going together to church and culminated with a special lunch cooked by Keith. I was truly fortunate to have everything going for me: the abiding support of my family, two lovely children, a decent husband, and all of us in good health. The shortage of finances was always overcome with help from my parental home and careful husbanding of resources on my part. Keith's parents too had reconciled to our marriage and there were loads of my friends to socialize with. What more could I have wished for.

Some months later however, like water passing through one's fingers, Keith's mock goodness was evaporated and he became his usual nasty, mean self once more.

Dreading a repetition of the emotional upheaval of separation and reunions we had been through over the past few months, I decided to stay on and endure my misfortune. Therefore, each time there was an unpleasant incident (which was a few times a day), I avoided retaliation, overlooked most verbal irritants, and kept out of Keith's way as much as possible. 'So now you have become too big-headed, to bother about what I say, just because I came begging you all to return,' he would jeer. Just in order to maintain peace at home, and only for the sake of the children, I did all I could to keep him from creating unnecessary unpleasantness in the house. This notwithstanding, I was rarely successful and still shudder at the memory of the unforgettable long winter night when he returned from an official engagement intoxicated with a substantial number of drinks, and told me that as he was going to be out for dinner, we should dine and turn in without waiting for him. So it was that after tucking six-year-old Mark and seven-year-old Fiona into their quilts after having given them their hot baths and dinner, I sat down to wait for him. The ear-shattering ring of the doorbell accompanied by loud thumping of the door announced the homecoming of my intoxicated husband. With a pounding heart and shivering body, I ran to let him in lest the racket wake the sleeping children. As I slid the latch open, Keith burst in with full force, almost throwing me off balance behind it. 'What have you been up to? Why did it take you this long to open the door,' he yelled. 'It's so dammed cold outside and I have been bloody slogging my backside off for you guys… while you cool your heels in bed…' Then flinging the scooter keys and his helmet with a thud on the floor, he continued, 'Why have you put the children to bed? You know I want to play with them when I come home… I know you don't want them to be with me… you bloody woman,' he shouted on top of his voice. I tried to say something to calm him down so the children didn't get shocked out of their sleep, but he pushed me out of his way and continued blabbering. Before I could do anything, he hauled little Fiona out of her bed, sat her down in front of him and kept on hurling abuses at me. He gripped the shocked little girl with one hand; and with the other, pulled the covers off the sleeping little boy. 'Get up you idiots… don't you realize your slogging father has returned,' he shrieked. 'I want you both to see what I do to your mother.' 'Please be quiet Keith,' I begged, 'don't do this to the children at least. They are in no way at fault.' I was weeping; suffering at the trauma the bewildered children were being subjected to, but nothing I could say or do seemed to be able to stop him from yelling, I remember laying my head at his feet begging forgiveness for anything I may have done… if only he would leave the children alone.

He kicked my head with his leg, flung Fiona on to the bed, and grabbed me by my nightdress and half pushing, half dragging me, he flung me out of the door of the apartment. Barefoot, clad only in a cotton nightdress, I landed stunned and horrified on the ice-cold cement staircase in the middle of the night. With lightning speed, he slammed the door shut upon me and locked it from inside.

While I sat sobbing on the staircase, I listened in terror to him shouting abuses and threats at the children and me, 'If the two of you dare to let that bitch in, I'll hammer the daylights out of your bloody bones,' he shouted. 'Let that bloody blind bat go to her bloody parents… I'll see how long they keep that good for nothing shit,' he growled. Then, as suddenly as it had all begun, all was silent inside the house.

After what seemed hours of sitting on the icy concrete steps on that cold winter night, listening to the soft whimpering of my terrified children on the other side of the door, I wept the last tears I ever shed in relation to Keith's ill-treatment. Any feelings I may have nurtured towards my husband died a permanent cold death and I knew for certain, I had a real battle on my hands. Yes, this was a full scale battle; a battle I had to win, for my children and me: the right to live, the right to safety, the right to be happy, the right to love and be loved, the right to freedom, the right to care and to be cared for, and the right to be human. We had done nothing to deserve being subjected to such atrocity. We were going to fight for our own home, a peaceful existence, and dignity! I once again realized my tears were never going to be shed again; crying would from now onwards be left to others. We had suffered enough of this piteous existence; happiness would be ours from now on and whatever the cost, I promised myself, and in my heart to my innocent little ones that come what may, I would do all it took to live life on our own terms with self-respect and dignity.

As if by magic, a strange calm descended over me, and ever-present sense of chilling foreboding vanished, substituted by an unwavering strength, faith, and courage. I was really glad to have been thrown out of my own home; for at least that incident had pushed me beyond my comfort zone and I was once again endowed with the wings of courage. 'It can't get any worse,' I thought to myself, 'I am going to make all my decisions from today onwards! It's I who suffer, so how can I expect anyone else to feel the real pain that living in this way subjects one to? I am going to turn every stone, explore beneath every bush for an opportunity to lead the dream life of which I have always dreamt.'

The soft whispering of my offspring aroused me from my reverie. 'Mummy… Mummy, are you there?' 'Yes sweeties,' I whispered back, 'I am here.' 'Seems as if Papa has gone to sleep now, and we are going to let you in,' they wept. 'Don't cry babies,' I whispered back, their whimpers wrenching my soul as I sat on the hard cold concrete, praying the neighbours did not hear. I couldn't bear any more pity. 'Mummy,' came little Fiona's tinkling, wavering voice, 'Mark has found the key and now we are going to climb on the sofa and open the lock for you. So, don't worry, everything is going to be fine; we have checked Papa is fast asleep and did not wake up even after we pushed him hard… so just wait.'

My eyes wept tears of love and gratitude, my heart swelled with joy and tenderness for these little darlings! They, at this tender age were moving heaven and earth to ensure my safety and here I had been subjecting them to such sheer emotional and physical hell every minute of their lives. 'Please be careful,' is all that I could say while I listened at the other side of the door to the sound of dragging furniture and the clicking of the latch. However, even after the lock had been opened, the door still refused to open. 'Oh no!', exclaimed two disappointed little voices; 'he has even latched the door from the top! Even from the top of the big sofa we can't reach that latch!' And then, 'I am putting this stool on top of the sofa Mark,' proclaimed Fiona's excited voice, 'then I will hold on to the stool and you climb on it and open the latch,' she instructed. I tried to discourage them from this risky operation but to no heed. 'Mummy, we can't leave you out in the dark and cold all night, and perhaps Papa will not allow you in tomorrow morning either, and what will we do without you Ma?'

After a few heart-stopping minutes, the door was opened and both of them nearly carried me indoors and we all huddled together under the covers and slept till the alarm woke me up in just a couple of hours to cope with a new day.

For me a new day had dawned and I was a changed woman, but for him, nothing had changed. He had probably no recollection or did not wish to remember his inexcusable conduct of the previous night. As for the children and myself, we had resolved, without putting into words, to keep it to ourselves.

It was typical of Keith that, following an episode of such extreme misbehaviour, he was exceptionally amiable to us all for the next few days. That is how it remained until the next round. As far as I was concerned, 'I would make the most of life as it came,' I declared to myself, and, henceforth, I let life take it's own course, keeping a sharp eye on opportunities that might present themselves. I got the children to help me with most of the things I could not manage on my own, and soon the three of us became extraordinarily independent, making fewer demands upon Keith, and with fewer responsibilities, his mood was better till he saw through the arrangement and his anger returned. 'So, now you think you can manage without me,' he would bellow, 'you want everyone to know I don't do anything for all of you.' Ignoring countless such taunts and ranting, I carried on till one day he threatened to hit little Mark with a hockey stick. I thereupon calmly told him, 'If you do that, then I will hit you back with it.' 'Ho, ho,' he sneered, 'you are as blind as a bat; you won't be able to get at me.' 'Well, I will hit you once you are asleep,' I replied, meaning every word. He laughed sarcastically and let the matter drop but, sadly, Mark told me many years later, that in my absence, his father had hit him with a hockey stick on his knees and threatened to break his legs if he ever dared to tell me about it.

It is impossible to weave into this narrative the day-to day atrocities of our existence, so I leave it to the reader to comprehend the type of life I lived. And to help your imagination to come close to my reality, I would like to mention here just a few additional challenges of my then existence!

My dear husband was again out of a job. I had no idea where the money to lavishly entertain his friends and himself came from. He was dishonest to the core and invariably had a new lady companion to keep him in good spirits. Drinking was a regular affair and how he managed to obtain a bottle of rum was of no consequence to him; he was forever ready to offer a meal to anyone who was willing to bring along a bottle. I had given up trying to talk sense to him regarding this, and instead, made the most of these frequent occasions as Keith would cook for his so-called good friends, and in the bargain, I myself got the advantage of a cooked meal and company. Once the evening was over, I would have to face the accusation of flirting with his friends.

However, as a love hungry human being, these evenings did provide me the opportunity of deriving emotional support. Although flirting had never been on my mind, I did very naturally become very fond of the most regular supplier of rum to my husband.

As I have mentioned earlier, Sunil was a sensitive and a good man, never failing to provide much-needed support at the worst of times. He too seemed to like my company, enjoyed my attention, and was wonderful with my children, and long before I realized it, my agonized mind assigned to him the image of an ideal husband.

It remained like that for a long time; I had his company to look forward to, his patient hearing of my travails and disgust at what I had to go through everyday, and his reassuring manner that lent me the emotional strength to endure Keith. This emotional attachment became a mental pillar of immeasurable strength that helped me shield myself from the constant excruciating pain in my life and the strength to battle my way out of it.

At this juncture, the future held only the hope of the children one day growing up into good citizens and being able to take care of themselves. However, with the nature of their childhood which adversely affected their studies and Mark having to frequently miss school due to severe asthmatic bouts, this seemed a long distance away. My aerobic classes too had dwindled to two students and a single class.

The acute stress took its toll upon my health, and my skin disorder aggravated, and in addition, I was bedridden for three months because of an irregular heart beat and general debilitation. I tried taking it easy, fully aware that I needed to be in excellent health to enjoy a good life. I therefore tried taking naps during the day when I was alone, but eventually had to bring an end to this because of the strange and frightening nightmares I would experience. I hated being alone when the kids were away at school or at play, and therefore busied myself with household chores, yet time hung on my hands. My inability to independently move out of doors and a hesitation to seek help from strangers had completely cut me off from the outside world. How then, was I to keep my mind sane through these lonely and vacuous times?

The answer presented itself in the form of prayer songs (*kirtans*). I would sit for hours listening to these from the Guru Granth Sahab over the cassette recorder. Of course, initially I couldn't understand much of this vast repository of knowledge, but listening to them repeatedly did help to give me the gist of some of the teachings of the great Gurus. My habit of taking everything literally, got me to gradually begin implementing these teachings in my life. The more I listened, the more I was convinced that my actions were responsible for my condition, that to improve my circumstances, that I must put in all the effort, and if I truly believed in what I was doing, God would help me accomplish what was desirable, and, if my efforts were not ultimately for my good, God would ensure that nothing would fructify. I therefore began to consciously search out the good that would temper my apparent misfortunes. This idea appeared quite ridiculous, 'How on earth could there be anything positive, given my present circumstances?' However, as I explored assiduously, determined to locate what the wisdom claimed, I soon had a long list of positives.

My marriage to Keith had given me two beautiful children, my own home, and the opportunity to manage life independently. His vindictive ways provided me with a wonderful opportunity to taste the bitter sweetness of economic independence and pushed me to becoming the first, probably in the world, visually impaired aerobic instructor. My horizons had expanded a hundredfold, following my entry into the outside world. I had gained confidence and my capabilities been demonstrated to many. I met innumerable people and my knowledge had continually grown. Keith's friends were now mine too; in fact some of them had become my life support, among them, Angelina and Sunil. I actually learnt to sit down and count my blessings and each element I listed made me feel happier with myself. When I began listing the negatives in my present life, there were just a few I could discover. These internal deliberations provided the daily dose of motivation and inner courage that helped me through those dismal times. As far as I could, I consciously dwelt on good things in my life, and these endowed me with immense inner tranquility and helped me to get through distressing situations.

I had realized by then that feeling depressed and unhappy did nothing to ameliorate its causes. The only way life could be transformed was to change my own thinking, and I kept working on this. I learnt to disregard pain and embarrassment, shortages and threats. I taught myself to enjoy it when sun shone and to lie low when storms raged; I learnt to swim with the current until I found the right moment to change course towards my goal. Above all, I did all that was within my power to better our condition, and left the rest to God. I also stopped worrying about what people would think or say, always remembering my mother's words: 'Elephants continue on their path, even though dogs continue to bark and snap at them.'

All this was difficult to execute because it required a huge amount of courage, discipline, and patience. It required great determination to remain unperturbed and follow through this approach to withstand the strong negative reverberations from the surrounding world. So long as the children were not threatened, I turned a blind eye and a deaf ear to every negative word and action that I was confronted with. I no longer struggled to pretend that all was well with our marriage, nor tried to suppress my protest against his unjust treatment. Gone were the days when I suffered in solitary silence. I now respected myself enough and loved my children sufficiently, so why did I have to crave to receive these from others.

Days moved along, zigzagging between intense moments of anger and frustration to wonderful moments of joy and pleasure. While from deep within I kept a sharp eye for the 'change' which Guru Nanak said was undoubtedly inevitable... 'Worry solely about that which is not destined to happen,' says the blessed Guru, 'because in the way of this world, nothing can escape change.' Having been brought up to believe in these words, the ardent expectation of 'change to be only for the better', journeying from this cheerless state, towards a better tomorrow, buoyed me on.

While I thus patiently awaited the fruits of the magic wand, the dawning of 1992 ushered in the wonderful news that Sandy was stepping into matrimony. We were to welcome into our family the charming and helpful, warm and affectionate Rachna. It was one of the most wonderful times of my life and the four months that were spent preparing for the big day and the wedding itself completely shut away all my misery.

Suddenly there was so much to do that I have only the faintest memories of Keith's activities. He sort of faded in and out of my days and nights, and as the wedding drew closer, along with the kids, I stayed at my parents' home.

Shopping, dancing and singing, were the highlights of those days besides the excitement of actually going to have a much longed for sister of my own. Fiona and Mark too were completely immersed in the excitement and freedom during the celebrations. It was their, one and only Mamu's (mother's brother) wedding and now they were to have Mami (his wife) to also spoil them. My enthusiasm knew no bounds, particularly given the depths of despair in which I had been plunged over the past nine years.

Remarkably, before the euphoria of the wedding had time to melt away, the opportunity of visiting Frauke in Germany suddenly fell into my lap. Miracles do happen; I spent exactly Rs 1900 for a 3-month holiday in Germany. My trip was a present from Aunty Frauke, to herself and me for an opportunity to once more spend some time together after sixteen long years of separation. It would certainly be an experience of a lifetime, for it meant travelling alone from Delhi to Bremen, having to change planes at Frankfurt, relying on strangers whose language I did not understand and actions I could not see. The one negative implication of such a trip was, to be away from the children for an unusually protracted spell. All this scared and worried me immensely, but the enormous opportunities and paid overseas holiday with my favourite aunt, and a godsend prospect of a getaway from Keith lured me into graciously accepting the wonderful offer, and this was further facilitated when my family volunteered to take complete charge of the kids during my absence.

On 2 July 1992, I took off on a Lufthansa aircraft, for an enlightening journey, with no alternative but to place my life and destiny in the hands of the unknown. I had an extraordinary time, and was completely blown away by the wonders that unfolded before me. The announcement that the temperature in Frankfurt was merely 15 degrees when I had been roasting on Keith's scooter at a whopping 46 degrees that very day set the tone. Then the pilot himself escorted me to the airport building and could not figure out where to deposit me. We went from door to door but no one seemed to want to take me in. Laughing heartily, he said, 'I think you'll have to come home with me sweet lady! No one seems to want you.' I grinned back, a little frightened yet now that I had leapt into the unknown, I was game for adventure, 'OK Sir,' I said smiling confidently, (feeling far from it), and enquired where he lived.

He was of course just joking to pleasantly tide over the miscommunication; and soon after handed me over to a young lady who had in her charge a little Indian boy, who was also travelling alone. Driving through the much talked about Frankfurt Airport in a tiny electronic car, I was struck by the emptiness of the buildings. 'Is it a holiday today?' I inquired of my kindly escort. 'Oh no, it is Monday morning and we are working,' she responded in a slightly surprised tone. An hour later, my flight to Bremen was announced and I was once more escorted into the almost empty aircraft by the pilot himself, and once we were airborne, the co-pilot, came around himself with the refreshments.

'Aren't there any people in this country,' I wondered? And then as I walked out of the aircraft, it reminded me of Agartala airport. The village-like deserted and silent atmosphere of the airport dissipated all my notions of arriving in a highly developed country. 'Hello Penny!'

came the familiar, sweet, and yet almost forgotten sound of Frauke's voice, brought my reveries to an excited halt. As if by magic, the warm circle of her arms around wholly eliminated from my existence all that had come to pass during the past sixteen years. I was myself once more, the happy and loving me; the confident and carefree girl of yesteryears.

The sun was shining brightly, dribbling its golden warmth through the crystal clear atmosphere. The entire family, including Sabine and Uncle Surjeet were there to welcome me. It was a wonderful new world. I had never imagined anything like this. I could almost hear the beauty of the vast green fields lined with massive trees and the smooth, wide and traffic-free motorway.

We drove to Frauke's home in Guni's car, friend and neighbour of Aunty Frauke, who had brought her to collect me from the airport. Excited and touched by the warmth of my reception, the loss of my baggage by the airlines was of little consequence. The feeling of freedom and fearlessness I was experiencing was to me more than heaven on earth.

The initial four weeks of my holiday were spent catching up on the last sixteen years. We talked, we cried, we ate, and just enjoyed being with one another. Frauke and I had all the time to ourselves as her husband, Helmut, was away on a healing vacation. Just to bring you up to date with some of the happenings of the past years, Aunt Frauke and Uncle Surjeet had divorced, and a few years earlier, Frauke had married Helmut. Uncle Surjeet too lived in Bremen and Sabine had begun living independently. Helmut too had three daughters from his first marriage and the girls all lived independently, away from home.

So, with the large house to ourselves, we both did as we pleased. Ever so often, we walked arm in arm, through peaceful lanes lined with lush hazelnut trees, through the fields speckled with wild flowers, over the arching wooden bridge across a duck-filled pond to the local store. Otherwise we sat on the little balcony sipping coffee and listening to our favourite songs.

My stress rapidly melted away, and, apart from missing Fiona and Mark, life was perfect. The serene and secure atmosphere rapidly healed my broken spirit, and the urge to strive for freedom and happiness gathered strength. I conjured wild thoughts, such as: 'If only I could by some stroke of divine intervention, bring my children to live in this wonderland', or: 'If only we could be rid of Keith's rotten behaviour… if only…'. These would be almost immediately followed by intense panic attacks, brought on by the realization that I would eventually have to return to my miserable existence back home.

Not wishing to ruin these present joyous moments, I would hastily push these disturbing thoughts aside and focus on enjoying the immediate. For the time being, I was bent upon soaking up all the positive energy I could from the uninhibited enjoyment and relaxation this holiday had to offer.

Subsequently, after Helmut got back home, the levels of activity and fun rose considerably. Although he spoke no English and I, no German, we got on wonderfully from the very first day because Helmut made the most of a German to English dictionary to facilitate communication between us. A good thing that was too, otherwise, I would have missed the excellent opportunity of acquiring the extensive knowledge he had of German culture and about other subjects that interested me. A history teacher by profession, Helmut ensured I had an opportunity to see and experience as much as possible; even if this meant going out of the way, to get me to touch every touchable item that could be reached.

Guni, the next door neighbour, too spent a lot of her time with me. We often went cycling around Bremen on a tandem bicycle. In addition, she took me along to her parents' home in north Germany for a long weekend. Uncle Surjeet and Sabine too, whenever time permitted, took me sightseeing.

On one such occasion, Sabine and two of her friends took me out for the day, and apart from visiting a farm, where I rode on horseback, I tasted the most exquisite of Chinese cuisine. In-between, we stopped over at the water park, where I had a sort of tiff with the caretaker. He was most upset because I refused to follow the rule of stripping to my skin before I went into the hot room. To be in a swimsuit was as far as I would go, but to go about naked, like the others, was asking for too much. Most of the people, including my cousin's friends thought I was being over modest, 'Hey, no one is going to look at you,' encouraged Norbert, Sabine's boyfriend, 'we all have the same things, so you should not imagine you will be ogled.' Anyhow, I clung tightly on to my skimpy black lace costume, while the irritated caretaker continually nagged me to take it off. Matters became even more amusing and awkward when, some time later, the same evening we sat up most of the night, drinking champagne on tall bar stools at a roadside bar near Norbert's penthouse. With the contents of more champagne tumblers swirling inside me than I can ever remember, I virtually tipped off the high barstool, nearly falling to the floor. Noticing my condition, Norbert half carried, half dragged me to his penthouse for the night. Sabine was still at the bar with some other friends and had said she would follow us later. Although half drunk, I was still sober to be worried about me being alone with this German surgeon in his house. He showed me into his bedroom and gallantly lifted my tee shirt to begin helping me off with my jeans. My fears appeared to have been confirmed. In drunken panic, I speedily stepped back, flung off his helping hands from the belt of my jeans, and said a hurried 'Thank you!' 'Oh dear woman,' he laughed, 'I was only going to help you change out of those uncomfortable jeans of yours and into my pyjamas.' Then he continued kindly, 'Hey, if you would like to use the bathroom, it is here to your left. I am now going up to bed... good-night, see you in the morning, dear lady.' Sighing with relief, I staggered towards the washroom. The next moment there was no ground under my feet, and I was kind of flying; and in the nick of time I felt Norbert's strong arms grabbing my waist. My flight was stalled in mid-air. 'This man is showing his true colours,' I thought, 'what does he think he is up to.' Kicking wildly, I tried to break free of his tight grip, when I heard him scream, 'You stupid lady, I wasn't going to rape you… you would have broken your neck… you just stepped off the stairs… If I hadn't caught you, you would have been dead.'

Returning to my senses, I realized my stupidity and immediately begged his pardon, and thanked him for saving my life. Thereafter, feeling shaken and foolish, I allowed him to help me to the washroom and then into my bed, without any further drama. Mind you, even so, I still refrained from changing into his pajamas, preferring to sleep in my own jeans, unconcerned with the discomfort. Besides, let me tell you, though, Norbert on this occasion had saved me from a fall down his penthouse stairs, I actually tumbled down the entire wooden staircase on my way out of a washroom at another garden birthday party. While I have never been particularly fond of hard liquor, I loved the bubbly German champagne, and guzzled down glass after glass and before I knew it, I would be swaying and high. Lots of champagne, lots of trips to the washroom, lots of wooden stairs, in combination with high heels and a happy heart, in conjunction with my sightlessness… and I must thank my stars that I survive to tell the story.

I could probably never adequately express in words the amazing personal turnaround these ninety days in Germany wrought on me. It became difficult to understand why I had for so many years, been subjecting myself to an almost inhuman existence. When there were limitless possibilities for the taking, why hadn't I even tried to look beyond the spectrum of growing up, marrying, and bringing up children, and thereafter, awaiting death? Thirty-three years of my life had gone by during which I did have some accomplishments to my credit; but these now appeared to be a mere trifle. Suddenly, now I began to see that the sky was the limit and the stars could all be mine, I simply had to pursue them. Destiny had played its part by revealing the unlimited bounty available. It was now my turn to act and garner it. My mind was made up; I would do whatever to realize my dreams.

On 19 September 1992, I landed at the Delhi Airport loaded with 60 kg extra baggage of clothes and shoes. The battered, frightened, and insecure Penny had transformed into a smart, confident, self-assured, and sparkling individual.

We, the children, my parents, Sandy and Keith, drove to my parents' home and stayed on for the night as there was a lot to catch up on. Besides, as the parts of the family I had left behind had been staying there during my absence, it was the natural thing to do. The next morning, when I asked Keith about my returning to our house, he answered sheepishly, 'I will first have to make the house livable as I have been living here since you left. It may be a good idea for us to continue living here for some time as I don't have a job either.'

Shocked and enraged at his taking everything for granted, considering that our relationship had already been on the verge of breaking down twice, I could not help flaring up. 'What have you been doing all these months?' I demanded to know. 'I refuse to return to living here again. Under no circumstances do I desire to put everyone through the nightmare of the past. Let us go home and I myself will find work if you help me, and together we will manage.' To this he had nothing to say, and instead, picked up his bag and keys and walked out of the door. None of us heard from him for months and therefore guessed that he had once and for all walked out of our lives for good.

After his departure, I heard about the difficult time Keith had given to all at home. Therefore, although his disappearance did evoke certain sadness, at least, we were at peace without his unpleasant and callous behaviour. Could my wish have been realized so easily? This could only be attributed to the fact that I no longer feared anything and he probably sensed that I wasn't going to fall prey to his bullying ways any longer, and without creating a scene, taken himself off.

Therefore, once more, for the third time, in four years, we were separated. Although life was most comfortable at my parents', I certainly missed our own home. Also, at the time I wasn't able to work out any future plans. Aerobics was no longer a dependable financial support. We were once again completely dependant upon my family for all our needs. With nothing much to do, time hung on my hands; the dream of relieving my family of the burden I had imposed on them haunted me continually. Besides, the false supposition that Aunty Frauke had brainwashed me into booting out my husband began to suffocate me. I had only heard of feeling lonely in company, but now this became my reality.

Then it all began once more. Keith called my kind-hearted mother again and said he wished to take the children out for Christmas shopping. Hearing about this, the poor darlings' faces lit up with delight and I wasn't able to deny them their birthright of seeing their father. I therefore dressed them in their Sunday best, and sent them off to meet him. After what seemed a lifetime, they returned cheerfully, lugging armloads of gifts from their father. They were both beside themselves with delight, as showed us with pride, shoes, clothes, and other trinkets their father had bought them. 'You know Mummy,' they both cooed with pleasure, 'you know, Papa has completely changed. He says he wants us all back home with him,' they informed me, looking at me hopefully. 'Papa promised he will never be angry again, and will never shout at you or at us again. And you know, he was crying so much Ma.' By now they were both cuddling next to me; 'Please Mummy, forgive him just this last time...' they pleaded in their innocent trusting way. 'He has promised to God and to us that he will be very good forever.'

With a huge effort, I swallowed the dismay and anger I felt at this new trap. 'Let us see children,' I replied, unwilling to hurt the innocent little children, 'your father has to first come and tell me what he wants, and then...' Before I could say any more, they both pranced up and down with triumph as they went on, 'Papa will phone us tomorrow and then we will ask him to come and take us all,' they announced.

Two happy children slept that night and after they had left for school, I could no longer contain my dismay and pain. I sat in the chair next to the kitchen door in the dining room and wept my heart out. I felt totally defeated. I had lost the strength to hold back my tears and sobs, and my mother cried along with me, trying to soothe me, and the cleaning woman too sat consoling me. Thankfully, the others were away and so I was spared the guilt of hurting them too.

The evening found Keith in the house begging forgiveness all round and making grand promises once more. He was now self-employed and had established his freelance supplier business, earned enough money to support us... and just wanted me to give him this last and only chance.

For the sake of the children, I once more made an about turn towards a fresh beginning. With a huge effort, I wiped clean from my heart all that had ever occurred over the past decade, filled my entire being with fresh hope, and thanked God from the bottom of my heart for the wonderful change that had come about in our lives. So what if time and toil could result in a lifetime of happiness for us all, I was ready to completely forgive and forget. There must have been some grave mistakes on my part too and I therefore promised to do my very best to be an ideal wife and mother.

So exactly four months after our third separation, on 10 January 1993, following a tearful send-off from my parental home, the children and I accompanied Keith back home.

It felt great to be back to a cheerful and sparkling home. The children were like a pair of happy puppies, darting around the rooms in utter glee, while I breathed the sweet taste of belonging and freedom. We once more dined happily together, eating heartily the delicious meatball curry and rice along with papadoms that Keith had cooked in our honour.

During the weeks that followed, life was perfect. Fiona and Mark were as good as gold, and Keith would help me with some of the household chores before he left for work. After having finished the rest of the housework, I would innovate with food in the kitchen, and before I got a breather, the kids would be back from school. Lunch would be followed with homework time, when my mother would come over to help me manage the children's studies. Then sharp at 5.00 in the evening, the kids would waltz away to play at Swati, the housing society where my parents stayed, to return home with their father on his way back from work. Thereafter, he would help me with getting them their dinner followed by bath and bed.

Then, one beautiful spring morning, about two months after our reunion, Keith returned from his early morning school bus stop trip for the kids and instead of helping me around the house, settled himself on the folding bed in the children's room with his cigarettes and newspaper. Pleasantly surprised at the prospect of having him home for the day, I generally enquired, 'Are you taking the day off today?' Flinging the paper on the bed he yelled, 'What the bloody hell… can't you leave me alone… you want me to go on slogging my ass off for you forever.' Shocked at this unexpected outburst and saying no more, I picked up the broom and began sweeping the dining room.

A few minutes later, he attempted some sort of an apology, 'I have to go late today, and that is why I was lying down… I didn't mean to shout at you… I am sorry.' His sudden change of behaviour had planted the icy hand of anguish and despair in my heart, and a pronouncement of the beginning of the end. What would the end be like? I couldn't envisage it, but I knew for certain that this man was never going to change. This was the last time; the children and I were being treated like a bag of toys, to be shuttled around to satisfy Keith's whims and fancies. From now onwards, I vowed, we would live life on our own terms.

Though I said and did nothing in response to him, life soon slipped back into the old pattern. As long as Keith was home, the danger of being shouted at, being hit and pushed was just a breath away. If little Mark spilt a grain of rice while eating, a slap accompanied by abuse would be inevitable, while he would go out at midnight to run errands for ladies in the neighbourhood. Therefore, in order to keep uncalled for unpleasantness at bay, I began to train Fiona and Mark to help me with things I couldn't manage myself. They took turns to go to the market next door for minor purchases, and sometimes acted as my escorts when serious shopping was required to be undertaken. Fiona was a well-accomplished shopper, but there was certainly much more entertainment when it was little Mark's trip to the shops. He would return singing and swinging what he had bought, which often resulted in an enforced omelette lunch. Then, on trips when he was my lone escort, his sense of responsibility urged him to walk ahead of me, while keeping a tight hold of my hand. When we had to negotiate an obstacle en route, he would halt in his tracks, step directly in front of me, lift up my dress, and instruct me to jump. However, all said and done, they were the most precious and well-meaning darlings in the world. How my heart bled when they were ill-treated at the hands of the man who was their biological father.

For the present, no opportunity was presenting itself to enable us to make the required change in our lives, so I continued to pass the time dreaming of the ideal man we all needed to provide the love, care, and support for which we yearned; the unafraid moments of laughter and carefree childhood my children deserved. It was I who had brought them into this world, so it had to be me who must shake heaven and earth to bring true happiness into their lives.

Day by day, I felt my courage growing, as I now openly defended them from their father's unjust lashings. In doing so, I often found myself screaming back at him. I will never get over the horrifying night, when I had to lock their bedroom door while they slept, to protect them from being harmed by a drunken father and his equally inebriated acquaintances.

Though I had decided to better my situation and had turned into a fighter, life would sometimes seem so unbearable that I would catch myself contemplating poisoning the children and myself. Then, one evening, the actual breaking point arrived, triggered off by a continuous bout of taunts, abuses, and threats from Keith. No, there was no particular reason that evening to have triggered his nastiness, but he went overboard with it. I couldn't stop my tears from involuntarily overflowing as I was going about fixing the evening meal and setting out the kid's clothes for school for the following day. Tormented by their father's conduct, Fiona and Mark too went about their evening schedule in a frightened hush. Seeing them smothered in this way, I tried hard to control myself, but was unable to hold back the helplessness and hopelessness that flowed from my eyes that evening. They dared not come to console me, realizing that if they did, it would only further aggravate their raging father. 14 September 1993 thus witnessed me weeping through the night with Keith relentlessly hurling all manners of vile abuse as he drank away. I must have dozed off sometime in between, because the shrill sound of the alarm jerked me back to the dazed horror of reality. It was morning, time to get up, so, as usual, I made tea and got the kids ready for school. Then, as I stood combing Mark's golden-brown hair, Fiona said, 'Mummy, I am going to stay with Nani from today. If you and Mark want to go on staying with this man, you can do so; but I am not coming back here.' Surprised and saddened by this declaration, I looked at Mark, wondering what his response would be to his sister's statement. 'I will also stay where Fiona does,' he announced, 'and anyway, Papa is always beating and shouting at us, so what is the point of staying here.' 'Every time he says he will not drink, he will not hit us and shout at you, but in a few days he is doing just that,' sobbed Fiona as she pulled on her socks. 'And, remember Fiona, last time he promised us that he would now change forever? But he remains the same,' said Mark sniffing. I was silent throughout this very sad discourse, wondering when this agony would come to an end. 'Are you sure you want to go away for ever? We can't keep going away and coming back, as we have been doing all these years,' I reminded them. 'Both of you can go to Nani's house for a few days and then come back and by then he will be OK,' I suggested. 'We are not returning,' was their unanimous verdict.

Once the children had left with their father to catch the school bus, I tried to lie down to get some rest, but the tears were back again. There seemed no way out of this... If I left him again and returned to my parental home, history would go on repeating itself and I had no strength to go through it again any longer. I could not find the courage to end my own life; neither did there seem to be a way of going to live independently minus Keith. The first step to independent living was economic independence, which meant I would need to work. What kind of work would I be able to get anyhow? I was blind, had no qualification, no training, aerobic classes did not fetch a regular income, and I was completely out of touch with music. The only other option that seemed available was to become a housemaid. If Muni (my mother's housemaid), could raise her nine children doing this, then why couldn't I? I would take the children to a distant place... I could rent a *jhuggi*, the kids could go to the government school, and we would at least be able to be live together sharing love and peace.

Such were my musings when I was startled by the angry thumping of the door and the shrill ring of the doorbell. Keith was back. As usual he marched in, flinging his helmet on the floor and the scooter keys on the sofa. 'Stop your bloody mewling,' he snarled, 'I have had enough of your crocodile tears all these years. That is all you can do, and you enjoy disgracing me in front of everyone. I can't take this any longer,' he yelled. I stood still in the middle of the large room, wondering what to say, or do. When he raced towards the balcony door threatening, 'I feel like breaking my head...' Panic-stricken at this new violence, I ran blindly towards the spot where I heard him to stop him from injuring himself. In the next instant, he grabbed me by the shoulders and tried flinging me on to the floor. I must have tried to prevent the fall and in the process, it was he who had landed onto the floor instead, with me on top of him. In a mad frenzy, I sat screaming on his stomach, grabbed his throat with both my hands and... a loud thundering on the door accompanied by the sound of the lady from next door brought me back to my senses.

Trembling, I rose to my feet, dragged my shaking legs towards the door and opened the latch. 'Are you alright, Penny?' she enquired, without attempting to come in. 'Yes,' I lied, 'I am fine.' The spell had been broken, I got down to dragging myself through the routine housework and Keith went over to his folding bed and newspaper in the kid's room as if nothing had happened. An hour later, the doorbell rang once more. It was my mother. A very odd time for her to visit, I thought. 'I had come down to the Mother Dairy for milk,' she explained, 'and thought I would drop in for a cup of tea with you guys.' While we sat drinking tea in the drawing room, Keith quickly dressed, and with a casual 'bye' to us, left the house.

Once he had gone, my mother asked me about what had been going on since last night? 'Nothing much,' I assured her, 'just the usual spot of normal disagreement that inevitably occurred in a house.' 'Don't try to hide things from me. Your neighbour called me some time back and told me that things were very bad between you and Keith.' I remained silent, not wishing to upset her any more, but she went on, with anxiety growing in her voice, 'She said they have been hearing all that has been going on here since last night, and that she felt she must inform me of the situation. In fact, Sandy should be arriving here any moment, and we will take you back home for good once and for all.'

'I am not going anywhere,' I declared, 'because in a few months someone or the other will coax me into reuniting once again. I can't bear it any longer. Let me cope with my lot however I can, please. I will manage somehow or the other.'

By then, Sandy had arrived and hearing my plea assured me, 'Now onwards, no one is ever going to send you back. You and the children will stay with us for good, you have my word.'

15 September 1993 witnessed us once again packing up for my fourth separation from Keith.

I once again took shelter in the love of my family, and especially in the heartwarming welcome and empathy of my dear sister-in-law, Rachna. In a short while, I had set up our mini home in the third bedroom at Swati. I knew for certain that this was definitely the end of the last and final marriage-saving attempt I would ever need to make. These trials had lasted for five long years and had taken a heavy toll on both my emotional and physical health, resulting in deep emptiness and painful scars. Thirty-four years of my life had elapsed and I had nothing to be proud of, excluding Fiona and Mark. Life had begun disbursing adversity to me very early, and I had fought to keep myself from surrendering to the threatening gloom, by hanging on with all my might to whatever shred of positives I could find. For the moment, however, I could only feel a vacuum engulfing me, nothing to look forward to, no direction to take; simply a dead end. Life had left me stranded in the middle of nowhere while the world strode rapidly along. My dreams too seemed to have become irrelevant in the face of my countless failures. Everything had suddenly taken on the garb of negativity, listlessness, and irritability. I vented my frustrations upon my children, developed a constant low fever, my mind felt numb; I had eventually seemed to have given up. Nothing seemed to attract my interest till one evening, Sandy was playing some new Hindi film music, and said, 'You must listen to this; you will really enjoy it,' he said, and I did enjoy it immensely....

The song, 'Choti si aasha' was from the film *Roja*. It said, within a tiny heart lies a tiny hope. The hope of flying in the sky, to touch the stars and the moon. To have the clouds wrapped around her and then to tie the whole world with her braid. The lyrics had the immediate effect of bringing back my own focus on to my buried dreams and my hopes lit-up afresh. This got me back to deriving encouragement and strength through my Gurbani cassettes. Eagerly, I began to spend most evenings with my children and their friends, playing along with them their crazy outdoor games. My dreams too emerged from hibernation, and I found something to look forward to in the form of the arrival of Rachna and Sandy's baby.

These positive changes in my outlook were accompanied by excellent opportunities for me. A stranger by the name of Mr Vikram Dutt, visited me one evening with an invitation to go to Calcutta for the Disabled Peoples' International (DPI) conference as a resource person for the 'Sports and Fitness' session as the expert on aerobics. My first reaction was of suspicion, because I had no idea of who this man was, and also because he insisted upon my travelling with this group of participants from Delhi, among whom I knew no one. I voiced my discomfort to Mr. Dutt, to which he gave an empathetic smile, 'Don't worry Preeti; we will all be there to look after you. Besides, your friend, Anuradha Mohit from NAB is also going.' With a very encouraging 'You must go,' from Sandy and an assurance of living arrangements with Anu, I shakily agreed to the supposed ordeal.

Then, just before I was to leave for Calcutta, my 'twinkle star' was born to Rachna and Sandy, in the form of an enchanting baby boy. As I held him for the first time, I knew my life was now to be one of hope and glory.

Swaying between inhibition and nervousness and shivering with uncertainty and cold, on a fairly cold November morning, I hurried along with Sandy as he escorted me to New Delhi railway station. I was to board the Kalka Mail for Calcutta, along with a large group of other unknown disabled participants. The thought of a 24-hour journey scared me stiff: how would I manage with so many complete strangers? My fears however vanished when I was greeted by the cheerful voice of a gentleman on wheelchair, followed by many other enthusiastic 'Good morning Preeti' emanating from every direction, I knew I was headed for a rocking time!

As a resource person, I had the privilege of staying at the Taj Hotel and as luck would have it, I was to be the lone occupant of the luxurious room. The overwhelming experience of meeting 300 persons with various disabilities and the limitless admiration and accolades I received, reinstated my lost self-esteem and confidence. I returned home with scores of friends and admirers; plus an offer of employment!

Mr Vikram Dutt accompanied by Anuradha Mohit, visited me again to motivate me to join the National Association for the Blind, Delhi, to teach typing and aerobics to the blind children at the school. Overjoyed but once again scared, it took some counselling to get me to take the plunge. I would have to travel by chartered bus, a distance of 22 km, cross the main road to the institution and thereafter, in the evening, find a way to board the bus back home. In addition, the salary was a paltry Rs 1,500 but I had to begin somewhere, and given my qualification and starting at a job at the age of thirty-four, I probably should not have expected more. The money would only pay for my travel expenses plus my clothes and toiletry.

Anyhow, on 2 February 1994, I joined my very first job. I had no mobility skills, (the art of using the white cane), and so for the first two days, Daddy accompanied me to the NAB, and on the third I made the journey on my own. The bus driver and his helper assisted me in stepping off at the right spot, and one of the assistants from NAB, came to help me cross the road and get to the school. I would ask someone from the NAB, to help me board the bus on the return journey after work, where someone from the family would receive me at the housing society gate.

Remember, mobile phones were unknown in India at the time, and you can imagine my plight when people forgot to come for me. The first time I was forgotten, I stood for a long time wondering what to do and then asked for help from a passing cyclist, who gladly obliged, though not fully comprehending why I had asked for his assistance. Yes, I informed him of my blindness, but I think he thought I was joking. The sheer frustration of frequently being forgotten on the roadside, I even unsuccessfully tried my hand at using a white cane, but soon gave up the whole idea as my alignment usually went out of step.

Well, somehow, I would manage to get myself to NAB every day. I began by teaching typing to the blind children, but ended up learning and later teaching the use of computers to them. During the very first few weeks of working, I had made loads of new friends, spent busy days, and had some money to call my own. It was a huge world out there: so much was happening and so much more could be done. I felt like a little bird that had been let out of her cage and was flitting from branch to branch, and then from tree to tree. There was so much to experience that the bumps I suffered and the silly mistakes I made as a result of my blindness coupled with ignorance of a professional set-up, only spiced up my days. Rather than feeling the usual embarrassment at walking into the wrong room, mistaking the window for the door, and bumping into the pillars and walls, I laughed at my own goof ups. I asked everything and everyone that made a noise and moved, for help, and nearly died laughing when I realized it was a dear cow to which I was saying, 'Excuse me, can you help me.' Well, I had lost most of my old friends, but one day, for old time's sake, and for the soft corner I still held for him, I telephoned Sunil. He did not sound overly enthusiastic about my call, but the news of my having taken up employment did add a note of astonishment to the normal monotonous tone he used when speaking to me. Thereafter, my calls were received with greater attention and interest by this man whom I now loved. Strangely, although aware that this love was one-sided, and there was virtually no chance of it ever being otherwise, I adored him with all my heart and kept in touch as often as I could. The charm of this 'one-sided love' attachment became the fuel for my existence, providing me with the enormous inner power it took to live through those difficult days. The power of love, it is said, can make miracles happen, and I guess that's true.

However, through one of my regular phone calls to Sunil, I learnt of the new business he had begun. His company had taken on the marketing and sale of pickles. 'What do you pay the salespersons?' I inquired. 'Four rupees and fifty paisa per bottle,' he replied dryly. 'Can I sell them too?' I asked, seeing an opportunity of making extra money and keeping in close touch with the man I loved. 'Yes, certainly,' was the now interested answer, 'I will bring you a few boxes and will pay you the commission on whatever you sell.'

The sale was on... I sold pickles to everyone that I could find: neighbours, colleagues, friends, and family. In addition, I lugged a bagful of twenty-four 400 gm glass bottles to every kitty party I could wiggle my way into. I went after all visitors and volunteers at NAB and ensured they bought my 'Oil Free' pickles. I even conducted a door-to-door selling campaign around our locality with either Fiona or Mark in tow to help me get around. By the end of a month and a half, I had single-handedly sold more than the four sales boys at Sunil's office were able to sell. You should have been around to see my ecstasy when Sunil called with the offer of the job of marketing manager for his company.

1 September 1994 saw me sitting beside Sunil, in his car, on my way to taking over as marketing manager for Granny's Pickles. It was unbelievable; in a mere span of seven months of having plunged into the supposed ordeal of full-time work, I had landed a prestigious job and got within arms' length of my life's dream. I was walking in seventh heaven and was now certain that God had taken over. Now that I had come this far, I would most certainly win the man of my dreams; it was now just a matter of time. I had already legally changed my name from 'Preeti Brown' to 'Preeti Singh' and was looking happily beyond to the final change, which was in the air.

Within a couple of weeks Sunil helped me further expand my natural flare for selling, and soon I was out independently going to the markets, shocking Indian shopkeepers.

I proved a revelation in the field; and soon a product that had been rejected by the market many times over, was prominently displayed without any charge by the relevant outlets, and found a place at many a dining table simply due to my innovative and natural selling skills. I personally promoted our pickles at fairs and outside shops. It was extraordinarily empowering to see my personality endorse the product so completely that we decided to market other products like popcorn and papadoms under the brand name 'Preeti'. So, along with the pickles, we launched popcorn with my signature branding the new products. The workload consequently increased substantially, and we needed more people to help.

Sunil highly recommended Ashwani, one of his former employees. Our office assistant extended the offer to Ashwani at a salary of Rs 2,500 per month. Although Ashwani was at that time going through a rough patch and required the money, he wished the company to pay additional travelling expenses for his motorbike, and I was therefore called upon to convince Ashwani to come on board.

The few persuasive words I spoke to him over the phone were, 'Ashwani, please join us from tomorrow on the terms that are being offered, and leave the rest to me.' My words had the desired effect and on 13 January 1995, after four months and eleven days of taking charge of the marketing concern, 'Ashwani' became a part of my team.

He was a quiet, committed youth of twenty-six, smart and gallant, good-looking, and well turned out. He walked with strength and determination, which were evident from the sound of his footsteps, denoting a firm and honest individual. His 'Good morning Ma'am', in addition to his meticulous work habits, total dedication, and reliability earned him my respect. Within a few days, Ashwani was my 'right-hand man'.

This was also the time when I was going about the nasty business of filing for a divorce. To find a good lawyer and to afford the fee was beyond my reach. I therefore had to approach a non-profit organization called 'Shakti' to help me. They referred me to another NGO, Shaktishalini, where a good woman by the name of Elizabeth put me in touch with an excellent lawyer, a well known high court lawyer in Delhi, Mr Sunil Mittal, who spontaneously agreed to help me out.

Simultaneously, I received the exhilarating offer of partnership in Sunil's business. He told me that special benefits were being offered by the Delhi Finance Corporation (DFC) for persons with disabilities; if I took a loan to put into his business, I could soon be a wealthy woman. I jumped at this opportunity; partnership in Sunil's business meant more money and also a closer bonding with the man of my dreams. As it was, things were looking up, and I had this strong feeling that from now on, only the best was in store for me. The children were busy with their school and play, and I had my plate full of work, which left me no time to cry over spilt milk. My day began at five in the morning, with teaching the aerobic class before helping the kids to get ready for school and readying myself for work. Then after a twelve to fourteen hour working day, there would be no time for anything beyond swallowing down my dinner and hitting the pillow.

Anyhow, with the passage of time, suddenly a strange change became apparent in Sunil's attitude towards me. It was initially manifested by his direct refusal to drive me to work everyday, followed by unnecessary and constant curt remarks and actions. Therefore, I requested Ashwani to take me on his motorcycle to the office and other places to which I needed to go. This was a nicer option, both relaxed and punctual, and in addition, it provided me the opportunity of building an excellent rapport with Ashwani and the rest of the boys in the office (I say 'boys' here as Aditi, my female assistant, had resigned from her job after working with me for about six months and now I was the only woman in the office).

Well, the processing of the loan proceeded speedily till it came to a roadblock because of the refusal of banks to open a current account in my name because I was blind. That eventually led to my taking the matter to the 'Human Rights Commission', who thereafter issued orders to the banks to permit me to open an account. This was indeed a major victory because henceforth, no bank in India could refuse a blind client the right to open and operate a current account.

Apart from Delhi, we launched our products in the neighbouring states on a shoestring budget, virtually single-handedly leading as well as spearheading the packaging, promotion, sales, and supply as well as collecting payments myself with the help of my team. It was very hard work but I thoroughly enjoyed every working moment. Walking the streets and markets in the burning heat of summer and the freezing cold nights, stumbling over stones and steps and facing pitiful remarks and glances only helped strengthen my determination. That in turn won me many prestigious National Awards like the Red And White Bravery Award for Social Work and the Rajeev Gandhi Manav Seva Award, to name a few. My story too was featuring in almost all the print and electronic media in the country. Encouraged by my success, and in order to earn some much-needed extra money, I attempted to experiment with writing articles for magazines and newspapers, and amazingly got published too. I use the word 'amazing', because I have never forgotten the demeaning episode of my essay notebook disgracefully being flung into the dustbin by my English teacher at Loreto Convent!

Incidentally, I would like to relate that though I was working really hard, I was still unable to fulfill my wish of earning enough money to support my children and myself without my family's help. I had therefore for the present to bury my desire to assist other disabled and underprivileged persons, and to find contentment in only partially rendering services to the disability sector. Thus, counselling and encouraging as I went along, freely sharing ideas and useful information with others, I dreamt of having my own Non-Governmental Organization one day.

The vision of owning our own home, where I would live peacefully with Fiona and Mark, motivated me to apply to the Delhi Development Authority (DDA) for the allotment of a low income group (LIG) flat.

As I swam the river of life with my mind fixed intently on my goal, each new hindrance only strengthened my strokes. Then, lo and behold, the next encounter with the unexpected razor sharp rocks cut into my soul! Sunil was getting married a second time and to someone else. This news snapped the imaginary string of hope and strength to which I clung. My folly had pitched me into sheer self-inflicted pain once more. I wanted to give up on life, but I couldn't. I must carry on; how could I break down? Breaking down and giving up would mean letting down my children, and also, how could I allow my family to see me in pain again. I therefore bit my lip, gripped my stricken heart with unseen claws of steel, and carried on as if nothing had happened.

Interestingly, at around the same time, I found out about Ashwani's broken love affair. The two of us shared an emotional bond; we had both been defeated in the game of love. As far as I was concerned, however, the question that faced me was how I could cope with one more failure in bringing my greatest dream to fruition. I seemed to be fighting a lost battle. Probably the world was right; I had no right to a fulfilling relationship because I was blind. I had fallen into the fire in the process of jumping out of the frying pan. I was probably destined to spend the rest of my life suffering in silence, watching the man I so loved, happily married to another woman. However, I simply had to earn a living for survival and there was apparently nowhere else I could do that, given my disability. Who would give me a job anywhere else? I was painfully under-qualified, was blind, and the social system was eventually getting the better of me.

It hurt; really hurt. To have no other recourse than working and living in close proximity to the man whose entire manner exuded the message: 'You will never be good enough for me.' Therefore, just in order to make this pain bearable, I found comfort in sharing my grief with Ashwani, believing that he might just understand my feelings at a time when we were sharing a similar experience. His too was a sad story: his girlfriend had left him for someone else, which had made him declare he would never look at another girl again. However, few would sympathize with a story like mine, yet his manner conveyed complete understanding. Our bonding grew rapidly, and the better I got to know him, the deeper became my regard and respect. Ashwani's capacity to care was exceeding my wildest imagination, and that with no strings attached. His fulfillment of my every official need and requirement without my having to ask never ceased to astonish me.

As our friendship blossomed, I began to almost envy the woman he would eventually take for his wife; although he most clearly proclaimed that he would never marry.

'What a shame,' I would think, 'some girl out there is missing the opportunity of marrying a wonderful man.' Then, late one Sunday evening, a huge but fantastic misunderstanding occurred. Ashwani was taking me home after having spent the day visiting common friends. This was a rare occasion for me and I had thoroughly enjoyed the outing. Therefore, on our ride up in the elevator to my home, I impulsively, out of sheer gratitude, hugged Ashwani, saying, 'Thanks for the wonderful day. I really like you so much, you are a great guy.'

As usual, he left without uttering a word, but things appeared weird the following morning. He arrived unusually late, his 'Good morning' was a mere mumble, and he appeared to be in a strange flutter. 'Hey,' I enquired, 'is something the matter?' No reply. 'Everything was fine till last night,' I mused. In total silence, he mounted his motorbike, as usual, and with a soft touch of his fingers upon my arm, indicated that I should climb up behind him. Swinging my leg across the seat to take my place behind him, I shook him by the shoulder and made another unsuccessful attempt to elicit the cause of his extremely altered, yet strangely cute attitude. Then, the next moment it struck me like a bolt: last night's farewell hug and compliment could have probably been misunderstood. My 'I like you very much' accompanied by the affectionate hug I gave him, seemed to have been taken for 'I love you Ashwani'.

'Oh heavens!' I groaned to myself, 'How could he even have begun imagining that I would fall in love with him?' Staggered beyond words, I nagged him till he confirmed my hypothesis. The rest of the thirty-minute journey to the office passed in total silence. 'How can this be possible? I am nearly ten years older than him,' I argued with myself, 'and am besides nearly a divorcee, mother of two teenage children, and a blind woman. He obviously deserves better than that. The thought of making Ashwani my life partner had up to that moment never occurred to me. I then wondered what will people think or say. Besides, we came from incredibly different cultures, and up to now having been associated with stylish men, how could I even dream of being coupled with so simple an individual? However, now that he thinks I have proposed love to him, I won't ever be able to disappoint him by an outright repudiation.'

Sliding off the bike after our quietest ride together, lost in our private thoughts, we threw ourselves into the business of the day. This day was however so unlike any other. I felt good and fuzzy, toying with the idea of actually becoming the 'lucky woman' and basking in the sunshine of Ashwani's devotion for the rest of my life.

'And why not?' I smiled to myself, 'Ash has in reality all the qualities of a perfect husband for which I could ever wish. How does it matter what people say, when these so-called people haven't been able to give me an iota of happiness or support; why in the world should I even bother in the least about them? In any event, I have to find an ideal life partner as I cannot end up being a dead burden upon my poor children. As it is, I seem to have taken far too long to be able to give them a decent childhood. I have to do something to take myself off their hands sooner or later. In addition, I was quite certain that Ashwani would be an ideal father for my darlings. We could then at last be together in our own home and love and care for one another and others around us. I was also well aware of the unconditional love and devotion I received from my family and therefore had a further reason to bring an end to the advantage I was taking of their loving goodness.

By the evening, I had made up my mind to ask Ashwani to marry me. As usual that evening we were the last to leave office, and once we were alone, I went up to him, 'Ashwani, will you marry me?' I asked directly. He sat motionless and said nothing again. This was probably getting too much for him. I repeated my question, not wanting to assume anything from his shocked silence. Probably guessing that ma'am wouldn't let him off without an answer, he did open his mouth: 'I must think it over before giving you an answer, ma'am,' came the gentle reply. Relieved that my hope was alive, we left office for home together.

From that day on, every morning, without fail, I enquired about his decision, to which all I got was the same 'I am still considering' reply. On the twenty-second day, before I could repeat my question, he asked smiling, 'Will you marry me ma'am?'

His decision cut the ground from beneath my feet! Up to now, I had only been imagining the enormous leap for which I had recklessly positioned myself. Now Ashwani's reply in the affirmative pushed me off my precarious perch, to trust him and God completely with my life and with the lives of all those associated with me. I was scared yet exalted; not many in India would have preceded me in this daring, cross-cultural flight. I could see a million trials and hurdles in our path, but was nonetheless, overjoyed and excited, I was certain that this was the great gift that God had been guiding me towards, through countless ups and downs, my hand was finally and firmly placed in His. From that day, to the day when we were actually able to tie the knot, Ashwani proposed and I said 'Yes' every single morning.

A few weeks later, I broke the news to my family, through my mother. As usual, she said she had already guessed, and was happy for me. Both my parents seemed to like Ashwani; so far, so good. Before long, however, the first impediment arose. Mummy advised me to let the children grow up with them, as she felt it might not be a good idea to uproot them once again. This came as a shock, as it meant, living apart from Fiona and Mark forever. Such a consequence had never occurred to me even in my wildest dreams. How was a mother to part, just like that, from her own most precious children? I was aware that the children were not being taken away from me, but it did signify a permanent separation, to say the least. This was not what I had struggled for all these thirteen years. Every single moment, from the time I had them, I had fought to find a loving and comfortable home for us together where I could nurture them within an uninhibited environment. To fearlessly enjoy together the hardships and the joys of a mother-children relationship, which up to now had been denied to us. Now however, as I stood on the threshold of my dream life, destiny was demanding its price in the form of the greatest sacrifice of all. Either I don't marry Ashwani, and thereby dishonour my love and commitment to him and deny myself the prospect of moving ahead in life, or go ahead, and leave behind my heart and soul with my little ones, hoping to reunite with them once they grew up. Obviously, the first choice would have been the more sensible one, I would have been in the world's good books to choose to sacrifice all and remain with my children, regardless of the consequences. It was however also the one which would have never pushed me to step out of my comfort zone and learn to fly with my own wings. Though it would be tough going, I had to move on; trusting Ashwani's love to give me the strength to bear the pain of the separation and to develop strong wings, on which I could one day teach my own offspring to fly independently. I had found out, of the importance of first securing one's own position, before succeeding in helping others. Therefore, with inexplicable difficulty and a very heavy heart, I decided to go ahead with the marriage and to leave the children with my parents. We would miss each other all the time; our family and home would be scattered and the children would now be left without both their parents. Anyhow, I decided to marry and live in as close a proximity to the children as possible, and learn the art of remote control parenting.

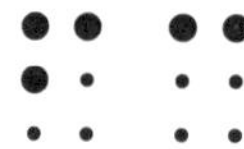

The following months saw both Ashwani and me work harder to take Sunil's business forward. Though I was to have been appointed a partner in the firm by now, nothing was being done. 'Let the company begin making a profit,' Sunil would taunt, 'What is there in a paper? We can have the partnership papers drawn up at any time. Anyhow, what will you do with a partnership? I will return the loan you have taken and you can continue working here as long as you wish,' he would say.

Upset yet helpless, we kept working, hoping the business would begin to become profitable, and with it, so would we. We therefore continued working almost twelve to fourteen hours a day under extremely trying conditions, and in addition, regularly attending court for my divorce, and prepared for our new life together.

My divorce came through on 1 August 1996 and we could be married in a month's time. The time had come for Ashwani to face one of the most difficult hurdles of all. Our wedding was planned for 15 September and around 20 August, he informed his parents of his decision to take me as his wife. Naturally, his parents strongly opposed the idea, and I don't blame them, but he said nothing beyond the fact that he would have to leave home to marry me.

We were finally married on 15 September 1996. The ceremony, followed by the wedding lunch, and Ashwani and I left for our small rented home in the Sancharlok Society, a short distance away from my parental home.

Entering our new home with mixed feelings, I stood watching the children explore their parents' one-room dwelling, before returning to their grandparents' home. 'Where will you cook Mummy? There is no kitchen here,' inquired Mark. Before I could reply, Fiona retorted in her usual bossy tone, 'Oh silly! Can't you see the gas stove here in the cupboard... and the dishes can be washed in the washbasin in the balcony.' Mark simply looked puzzled and said no more.

'How was I going to live without my little sweethearts,' I thought, trying my utmost not to let the lump in my throat, melt out of my unseeing eyes. Strange and painful thoughts rushed through my mind: 'What would become of our lives? Whenever I seem to successfully work a way out of one appalling situation,' I thought sadly, 'mercilessly, more complicated issues entrap me. Today should have been the happiest day of my life, but instead, I had brought upon my children and myself the absurd penance of separation!'

On one hand, I had finally won the man of my dreams, to live with, love, and care for, won peace, security, and respect, but there would be no complete togetherness after all. For the moment however, there was nothing I could do beyond folding my hands in prayer and seeking the strength to endure this test of time with courage and faith. This was probably the most soul-shattering suffering of my life and strangely and curiously, came enveloping the greatest gift I ever received.

Fortunately however, I was not alone this time, as I had my loving husband by my side. I was completely in accord with his declaration to not have any more children through our marriage, so Fiona and Mark never have any reason to feel abandoned or neglected.

However, now as I stood watching my children actually preparing to leave me and our home, the turmoil and pain within me was enormous and inexplicable. I knew they were very sad too, as little Fiona had been crying bitterly at the thought of having me gone. Although, they both had agreed to my remarrying, it must have been a great torture for them. I shall never forget Fiona's little weeping voice saying, 'Don't worry Ma; this is just a little pre-wedding crying. We will be fine with Nani.'

It however felt as if I had managed to rescue myself from a raging fire, but had left my children to fend for themselves hereafter amidst the flames. 'Whatever God does, is always the best for us,' and 'everything that happens, is always the will of God,' were the thoughts that lent me the strength and courage to stand resolutely by my taxing resolution.

The sounds of 'OK bye, Mummy,' jerked me out of my agonizing reverie and with an effort I jerked myself back to what was at hand: the very moment of our final goodbyes was at hand. I stood in the open doorway, bidding farewell to the blameless sufferers, with lips smiling and heart weeping, as they hugged and kissed us and ran off. An unutterable sense of loss engulfed me, as I slowly pulled the door shut and bolted it. All this while, Ashwani had been silently standing just behind me, but as I slowly turned around to where Ashwani stood after having bolted the door, I saw Sai Baba standing right there. (I am a totally blind woman, and I actually saw Sai Baba standing there.) At that very instant Baba, in His way, assured me of His unwavering presence in the garb of Ashwani and I knew then that I was on the right path. My journey was going to be a taxing one, but Baba promised to hold my hand firmly all along the way.

Our marriage was a great shock to everyone; including our colleagues. 'How long have you both been going around?' asked our colleagues. 'Almost a year,' I giggled. 'What fools we must be not to have noticed,' they groaned.

A week later, Ashwani and I left for Bombay to launch our products and on our return after a ten-day working honeymoon, we found a further change in our boss's attitude. His displeasure with Ashwani became more than apparent. His sole aim now seemed to be to get rid of my husband. Then finally, in April 1997, for no apparent reason, he terminated Ashwani's service, instructing him never to enter the office again. Although I was granted permission to continue working if I so desired, after such behaviour, this was out of the question. I therefore asked Sunil to return the Rs 2 lakh that the company had borrowed against my name, to enable me to leave too. Sunil agreed to give me post-dated cheques in the name of the financers, and after a delay of 18 days, the cheques were handed over to me. Besides, before I returned home on that fateful day, my supply vehicle had been removed from our home parking lot.

We were both out of work, our auto-trailer had gone, and we had no idea from where the money for the coming months' expenses would come. Placing our faith in God, we looked for a job and before long we were hired by the manufacturer of Granny's Pickles to independently market his product, as he too had fallen out with Sunil. This job too lasted just a few months, and on 1 December 1997, our services were terminated via an abrupt early morning phone call.

'You will of course get a job,' I told Ashwani, 'but I don't think it will be easy for me.' Ashwani had a computer and we began to hunt for some part-time work while searching for regular jobs. That too had to wait as I had committed myself to going to Madras to participate in a fashion show organized by the Ability Foundation. I had always dreamt of walking the ramp and this opportunity fell into my lap from nowhere. They asked me to travel by train, which I refused to do given the wastage of time and expected to be excluded from the programme, but, to my utter surprise, they sent me two air tickets enabling Ashwani to accompany me.

A dream come true once more: it was a fashion show where persons with disabilities were to model alongside professional models like the Miss World film star, Aishwarya Rai. At a later date, I was invited to model for another fashion show, where the famous actor from Bollywood, Rahul Dev was to be my co-model.

Well, climbing down the stage, we still had the challenge of looking for work awaiting us. A transcription job from the Rajeev Gandhi Foundation helped us tide over our current jobless month. Then, as luck would have it, I became pregnant. Though we both wanted to have the baby, Ashwani reminded me of his resolve not to have any children, so the pregnancy was terminated.

Caught between completion of the transcription work, going for the fashion show, hunting for jobs, having my pregnancy terminated, and managing the house, left us no time for any other worries or breast-beating. It was all happening in a flurry and before I knew it, I had a job with Katha, an NGO working in the field of education and publishing, as a public relations and revenue manager, which paid me as much as hitherto both our earnings combined had yielded. Sai Baba had kept his word!

Ashwani's parents had reconciled with us, and a cordial relationship was established. Fiona and Mark too were settled in the loving care of my family and we saw them as frequently as possible. My mother kept me updated about all that went on in their lives to afford me the opportunity of guiding them in my own subtle way. Ever so often, I would sit weeping with sheer helplessness at not being able to love and care for them both in the way any normal mother did, but deep down, I knew all would end well. 'But, when? How?' was the question uppermost in my mind, and the answer to this in my thoughts was: 'Live an exemplary life so that when the time comes, your children can follow the path you create.'

The beginning of 1998 heralded the excellent news of the allotment of a DDA flat of our very own. Another of my dreams had been realized, but this dream too presented a major hurdle. We had to make a payment of over 4 lakh to the DDA within a stipulated period, or forgo the apartment.

It is not easy to erase the memory of holding the allotment letter in our hands, sitting on the mattress on the floor of our one-room rented flat, and feel utterly helpless and disappointed. Nor can one forget the effort of silently putting the letter away, and going back to our regular business, secretly praying for a miracle to happen. Then, once more the will of God was at work. Everyone came together and pitched in the required cash: my parents, Sandy and Rachna, and even Ashwani's parents helped us to top up the amount we had been able to save in the past. Lo and behold, our dream became our reality, in the form of a beautiful three-side open, top floor apartment in Mayur Vihar.

These were truly miracles taking place; as many years ago, Ashwani and I had come to Mayur Vihar phase two to deliver a package and had stood wishing aloud: 'If only we could own a flat in this locality,' and now our apartment was in the exact location where we had wished it to be. It was crazy... exactly as we had imagined. A one-bedroom flat, on the top floor, compact and cute; it was all this and much more.

21 March 1998 witnessed our moving into our own home. I call it a miracle because on that very day, Ashwani got the job that proved the turning point in our lives. Thus, settled in our new home, with excellent jobs in hand, all our challenges for the moment overcome, we were now knowable to direct our energies towards relaxed hard work.

A couple of months later, a woman called Mamta and her husband moved in next door and became a close friend and my link with people in the colony. From her, I soon discovered that I had become the discussion point of the neighbourhood. People heard I was blind but not many believed it: 'She does all the housework herself and even cooks unaided, and, she does not look blind.' Amused by these reports, I continued to carry my cut vegetables across the landing to Mamta's door, for her to check them for unwelcome caterpillars, and, in return, she'd often come over to learn a new recipe or two to let me help her to cope with stress. I was happy and busy, with life's sweet and sour flavours that lent wings to time.

Ours was an ideal marriage, sprinkled with a few harmless tiffs. These were usually triggered off when Ashwani was unable to correctly match petticoats for the colours of saris I wished to wear, or his refusal to eat fruits and vegetables which I loved.

Well, I once more started taking the chartered bus and was assisted by many friends and acquaintances to safely get to work and back. In the office, I became aware that the initial admiration I received from my co-workers degenerated into a curious resentment towards me. This was probably because of my efficient performance at office, which probably gave my co-workers an inferiority complex. They probably felt that if I with my major disability stood at par with them, they should be doing much better as they were more qualified and able-bodied. Their resentment was expressed in various forms, some in the form of unsolicited sympathy while others went out of their way to find faults, and yet others pointedly ignored me or placed needless obstacles in my path. There were even some who actually made it their business to voluntarily do the work assigned to me, simply to demonstrate my incapacity to cope with it. Not being in the habit of complaining, I ignored most of these ridiculous actions and utilized my working time to the best of my ability.

Apart from working at Katha, I continued to work freelance with the disability sector. Then, in early August 2000, I was offered a position with one of north India's most prestigious eye hospitals. It was a pleasant surprise to be given the opportunity to head the public relations department of Dr Shroff's Charity Eye Hospital. Apart from public relations, I was drawn into fund raising, marketing, training, trauma counseling, and patient relations activities for the hospital.

In September 1998 I joined this fantastic organization along with my newly found assistant Gurdeep. Gurdeep was a huge asset in my success at SCEH, with her efficient, honest, sensitive, and dedicated support, to me and the hospital

The spring of 2002 brought the good news that Fiona's schooling had come to a successful end, and that she was joining college. Mark too was preparing for the high school examination via the National Open School. His health had in the end dissuaded him from continuing at regular school. By now, I had learnt to place my total faith in God's ways; to keep setting an example for my children, through my own actions, and to hope that the best would befall us.

My day usually began at 4.30 a.m. with the cleaning, ironing, and cooking in addition to my regular exercise programme, before I left for office at 8.00 a.m. I would be home by 5.30 in the evening and normally had the evening meal ready by the time Ashwani returned home. Following preparations for the morning and after dinner, I would fall asleep as soon as my head touched the pillow at around 10 p.m.

As I mentioned in passing earlier, in the course of the past few years, I have been awarded a number of awards for my work, including the prestigious Red and White Bravery Award for Social Work and the Manav Seva award. 'Mummy, why do you get all these awards,' asked my kids once in all innocence. I honestly wonder myself why did I receive such recognition. As far as I was concerned, I had done nothing special apart from simply doing my best to keep my head above water and remain happy doing so.

Then suddenly in the spring of 2002, I developed a slow fever along with severe body ache. Not willing to let ill health come in the way of our just stabilizing financial situation, I secretly popped pills to keep myself going, because consulting a doctor would mean absence from work, loss of pay, or perhaps losing my job altogether. 'Unthinkable,' I told myself, 'you have contracted a viral infection and it will sooner or later disappear.' I therefore dragged my aching body, swallowed painkillers as often as possible, and kept my troubles to myself. No matter how I tried to suppress my failing health, the fever persisted, my mouth developed sores preventing me from eating resulting in rapid weight loss. The pain stopped responding to off-the-shelf painkillers, my fingers swelled, and my energy level fell till I could barely manage to get dressed and go to work. By then, the alarm had been raised and I was dragged to a doctor's clinic which unsuccessfully treated me for everything they could figure out, including tuberculosis. By mid August, I had to move to my parents' home to be looked after. Everything had to be done for me; I could not even turn on to my side in bed, and the pain was devastating.

Eventually, some trouble was detected with my uterus and ovaries, and I was operated upon and the entire uterus was removed. Despite the surgery, the body pain continued to persist, worsening with every hour. Then further investigations revealed, SLE (an auto-immune disorder). A heavy dose of steroids was administered, following which the pain magically vanished; leaving in its wake, agonizing side effects.

After about six weeks of my surgery, I returned to our own home and there begun the solitary and treacherous journey to a painfully slow recovery. As I gradually recovered strength, the dosage of steroids decreased, but the disorder was there to stay said the doctors. 'How can I stop taking these dreadful medicines, if not rid myself of the disease?' I enquired. 'Keep fit, be as active as possible, and forget that you suffer from any disorder,' was the doctor's simple reply.

It was very well for my doctor to say that, but how was I to remain active with a weak and quivering body? I could barely hold a cup of tea steady for over a few seconds, so how was I to build up my strength to remain active? I had, however, to get on with life once again; the idea of remaining ill and dependant for the rest of my life was completely out of the question. I therefore once again prayed for the courage and guidance to get myself back into working order.

Then, slowly and steadily, I literally forced my weak and unsteady body and mind to resume the day-to-day work. With trembling limbs, I got back to cooking and shortly took up dusting and mopping, ironing and washing. Then, as soon as the doctor permitted, I resumed exercise, first by walking inside the house, then on the balcony, and as my legs gained strength, climbed stairs and cycled on the stationary cycle, till about six months later, I was able to return to my normal aerobic and callisthenic routine. Gradually, the pain that subsisted became bearable, but it was years before the stiffness stopped being a hindrance.

In the mean time, Ashwani and I bought our first car. It seemed to be unbelievable but it was true: 'Our own home, and now we had our own car.' Fiona too had begun working and Mark had completed high school and was training to be a dancer. Though challenges still remained, they taught me to swim with considerable ease.

In 2004, my parents moved to Chandigarh after my grandmother fell ill, while my children continued to live at Swati. On 21 January 2005, Fiona married Shubrangshu Banerjee, a very charming young Bengali. Remember, I was to tell you why I appreciated my childhood training in Bengali culture and language. Here it is... Fiona has married into a Bengali family and Mark too weds Mimi, a sweet Bengali girl this year. See, God made certain I was well-versed with the language and its culture much in advance.

Following Fiona's wedding, Mark found employment in Chandigarh and moved there to live with my parents. Finding the task of nurturing my children done with, I began searching for a direction to fill the void that was threatening to swallow me into a morass of depression and loneliness.

The golden hope of a reunion, (to live under one roof together), at the end of our struggles was gone forever; the growing distance to be our reality is something I have to accept. I now truly understood the meaning of the age-old couplet from my childhood, *'Pata tuta dal say...'* translating as 'the leaf broke from the branch, the wind carried it away; once parted, they have never met, they have travelled far.'

Thus to remain healthy, happy, and independent, constantly counted my blessings, and escaped from my terrifying auto-immune disorder, and found pleasure during free moments, in reading and writing. Never before had I been able to spare time for these passions given my pains and worries, so now I was pleasantly surprised at the joy I derived from them.

In December 2002, having been on leave for three and a half months, I rejoined the hospital, but as I feared, most of my responsibilities had been assumed by others. Anyhow, as I had learnt by now that no situation is permanent, I busied myself with whatever work was assigned to me. I, however, sensed that my full potential was not being utilized, so I took this up with all concerned. When all such efforts failed to elicit a favourable outcome, I assumed a 'wait and watch' mode, and at the same time, worked towards launching my own organization and practiced the art of writing.

At the workplace, I perceived a host of indirect negative comments and actions directed towards me. At that time, I was probably very vulnerable due to my prolonged illness, and tended to view everything in a negative light, and generally felt unhappy and disillusioned. I wanted to resign and retreat to the secure comfort of my home. My fighting spirit however, once more supervened, and I did whatever work I could lay my hands upon, and spent the rest of the time expanding my knowledge.

Then one day, I was invited to conduct a motivation seminar for the employees of the corporate giant Nestle, the success of which propelled me to add corporate training to my professional skills. Ever since then, I have become a full-fledged corporate trainer and have been training professionals at leading Indian corporate houses. My life was being transformed all over again; from my most recent professional and physical setback emerged the opportunity for my next directional change. The touching feedback I received and increasing demands for more, was proof of the excellent transformational quality of my 'Dream it, Do it' workshops. I witnessed extraordinarily positive turnarounds on the part of the participants at these workshops, and within myself, and accepted with great exhilaration and humility, the heart-warming ovation I received.

The earnings from these training programmes go towards motivation and personal development workshops for the disabled and underprivileged individuals through the work of my organization, *Silver Linings*.

My mission now became to inspire, guide, and motivate people all over the world to teach and share what I had experienced and imbibed and to help others discover and develop their own personal talents and experience a sense of joy and fulfillment. The broader world is such an all-encompassing and powerful entity, and I, but an ordinary individual with few connections, so I wondered how I could accomplish this lofty mission. 'Every drop counts,' my inner voice urged, 'one step at a time, one day at a time, and some day, you will a find way,' went the age old saying in which buzzed my head, as I wholeheartedly made myself available at every forum I could reach. I invited people home, went to friends and advised colleagues, delivered lectures and conducted workshops and training sessions wherever possible. I never missed an opportunity of being noticed by the media.

My efforts at increasing my reach and enhancing my income won me the privilege of being taken on as consultant by the National Opportunities Alliance to train teachers of their partner organizations, and to persuade, employers to hire youth with disabilities in their organizations. In addition, I was first appointed as the India coordinator and then nominated as a board member for the Combat Blindness Foundation India (CBF-India), a US-based organization, working in the area of avoidable blindness in the developing world.

In 2006, my happiness reached its acme with the birth of our little angel, Rudrangshu, our grandson. Now, our small family had begun stepping towards the next generation, Ashwani and I planned to buy a bigger home. Although the dream seemed lofty as the prices of real estate had skyrocketed; miraculously, in 2007 we were able to purchase our new house. Not many believe us when we tell them that the entire interior of our dream house has been designed by me.

Then, in early 2008, with the encouragement from family and friends began the journey of this book, a sincere endeavour to reach you, dear reader. Alongside, I wrote the content for my website as well and worked on a story for the 'Chicken Soup' series in addition to authoring a 'Hot Shot' recipe book in collaboration with Susan Vishwanathan, a scholar and dear friend.

Now I have stepped further into the unknown. I eventually gave up my job at SCEH on 25 February 2010 and have launched a new business venture called Silver Linings HR Solutions Pvt. Ltd, an executive search company. I have been joined in this by my brother Sandeep, and today, we have a fully- fledged team working with us.

I am one of the very few people who are completely happy and fulfilled, living life on my own terms. I seem to keep dreaming dreams, happily manifesting them into my reality, and moving on to the next bunch of dreams to chase. I have been fortunate in having succeeded in leaping into the unknown, in pursuit of my dreams and in the absence of the sense of sight, clutching on to the rope of faith, depending upon the wings of 'the other senses'. I can only pray that my story will inspire you, my readers to follow suit and tenaciously pursue yours in the same spirit of faith and enterprise.

About the Author

Preeti Monga is a trauma counsellor, corporate trainer, writer, aerobics trainer, public speaker, and director of Silver Linings Human Resource Solution Private Limited. Winner of various awards, Preeti was the first Indian visually impaired person to successfully clear the Aerobic Instructor training. Now a successful entrepreneur, she has been relentlessly working on equal rights for people with special needs and also counsels people on the benefits of healthy diet and living.